THE SCHOOL THAT'S OUT OF THIS WORLD

Hyperspace High is first published in the United States by
Stone Arch Books
A Capstone imprint
1710 Roe Crest Drive
North Mankato, Minnesota 56003
www.capstonepub.com

First published in 2013 by Curious Fox
an imprint of Capstone Global Library Limited,
7 Pilgrim Street, London, EC4V 6LB
Registered company number: 6695582
www.curious-fox.com

Text © Hothouse Fiction Ltd 2013
Series created by Hothouse Fiction
www.hothousefiction.com
The author's moral rights are hereby asserted.

Library of Congress Cataloging-in-Publication Data is available on the
Library of Congress website.
ISBN: 978-1-4342-6306-3 (library binding)
ISBN: 978-1-4342-6310-0 (paperback)

Summary: When John Riley gets on the wrong bus, he ends up at an elite
academy on an enormous spaceship, where his classmates are aliens, the food
is disgusting, and the penalty for failing exams is harsh. Can he show that he
deserves a place at Hyperspace High?

Designer: Alison Thiele

With special thanks to Martin Howard

Printed in the United States of America in Stevens Point, Wisconsin.
022014   008034

HYPERSPACE HIGH

CRASH LANDING

written by ZAC HARRISON • illustrated by DANI GEREMIA

STONE ARCH BOOKS™
a capstone imprint   www.capstonepub.com

CHAPTER 1

Morning sunlight streamed in through the window. With a groan, John Riley pulled the blanket around his head and rolled over. Killer aliens with hideous, venom-drooling fangs were attacking his spaceship. Any moment now, they would come crashing through the door. He pulled a blaster pistol from its holster. Let them come.

Somewhere close by, a voice yelled, "Are you ready, John? *John!*"

The words seemed like part of his dream. John couldn't help noticing that the aliens were now dressed like his mother.

That's weird.

"John, I *said,* are you ready?"

John frowned under the blanket. *Oh. I'm dreaming,* he thought. *Rats. And it was just getting exciting. . . .*

John's eyes flickered open. There was something he should have remembered. *Oh, yeah,* he thought fuzzily. He had to catch the bus for his first day at boarding school. But there was nothing to worry about; the alarm would wake him up. There was more than enough time for more sleep. *Maybe,* he thought, *I can get back into the dream.*

With a yawn, he closed his eyes and burrowed farther beneath the blanket.

The door crashed open.

"You're still in bed? The bus leaves in fifteen minutes and your dad and I have to get to work," John's mother babbled.

"What? Huh?"

"Get up! Get *up*! You're late!"

John sat bolt upright, flinging back the covers and blinking sleep from his eyes. "No I'm not. I can't be. I set the alarm clock."

His mom picked up the clock and peered at it. "*This* alarm clock? The alarm clock without batteries in it?"

A memory rushed back. The video game controller had needed fresh batteries while he was in the middle of a level. He'd taken them out of the clock and instantly forgotten as he rejoined the laser battle.

"Why didn't you wake me up?" he yelled, leaping out of bed and pulling his T-shirt over his head.

"Don't blame me, I've been shouting for the last half hour," his mother said quickly.

Frantically, John tugged on a pair of jeans and a sweater over his T-shirt. Precious minutes were wasted looking for a lost sneaker, which he found wedged behind the back of the bed. Brushing his teeth in the bathroom, he caught sight of himself in the mirror. Blond hair stuck out at bizarre angles. He couldn't go to school looking this ridiculous. Grimacing, John turned the water on full blast and stuck his head under the water.

"*Waaaaa-hahh!*" he screamed, as freezing water poured onto his head. "Awake, I'm awake, I'm awake!"

Grabbing his backpack, thankful he'd packed it the night before and that most of his luggage had been sent on ahead, John finally made it as far as the kitchen. He looked up at the clock: he had five minutes before the bus was supposed to come.

His dad was throwing papers into a briefcase. As he looked up, he said, "Sweet mercy, what is that thing? It looks like the creature from the black lagoon."

John's mom put a slice of toast in her son's hand and attacked his wet hair with a brush while he chewed.

"Or some sort of mutant," his dad continued. He was clearly enjoying the moment.

"Dad?"

"Hmmm, it's calling me 'Dad,' but I don't believe it. What have you done with my son, vile fiend?"

"You're not helping, Dad."

"Okay," his mother interrupted. "*I* wouldn't want to be seen with you, but at least you won't frighten small children."

"Thanks, Mom. I'd better go."

"Not so fast, disgusting thing," said his dad, rising from his chair. "Give me a hug."

"Bye, Dad," John said, hugging his father. He felt his dad slip some money into his pocket. "Thanks. I'll see you at break."

"My turn," said his mother, catching him in her arms. "I'll miss you."

John lifted his face to kiss her and saw tears in her eyes. "Come on, Mom," he said softly. "I'll be home in a few weeks."

"Are you absolutely positive you don't want us to come with you to the bus stop?"

John shook his head. "No way, Mom! I don't want to look like a baby." Secretly, John was worried that he might cry, too. He glanced at the clock. Three minutes left. "I'll call or email as often as I can," he promised, wriggling free. "But I have to run or I'll miss the bus."

Stopping only to wave to his parents as they climbed into the car to go to work, John tore out of the house and down the street toward the main road, where the bus would be waiting.

It'll wait. The bus will wait. It won't leave without me.

He remembered the letter the school had sent, telling him where he would be picked up. The words "PLEASE BE ON TIME" had been in capital letters and underlined.

John picked up speed.

Dashing around the corner, he saw the bus gleaming in the morning sunshine. It was sleek and silver and looked both brand-new and ultra-modern. A slim woman with a tall, old-fashioned beehive hairstyle was leaning against the bus doors and looking impatiently at an electronic screen in her hand.

"I'm here! I'm coming!" John yelled as he

sprinted down the road, waving, his backpack bouncing on his back.

At the door, he skidded to a halt.

"You're late," snapped the woman. "I'll have to make a note." She jabbed at the thin screen — a design that John had never seen before — with long fingers. *Very* long fingers, John couldn't help noticing. A lot like the rest of her. The woman was well over six feet tall and as thin as a pencil in her brown tweed suit. And with her hairdo adding almost another foot, she towered above him.

"S-sorry," he panted. "Alarm didn't go off." Getting his breath back a little, John looked up at her and almost stepped back in shock. The woman's hair was obviously a wig. A bad wig. He could see the gap where it didn't quite meet her forehead.

Aware that he was beginning to stare, he

looked away again. "I-I'll get on, then, okay?" he stuttered.

"That would be most excellent," the woman said crisply. "The departure window closes in twenty-six seconds."

Scrambling up the steps, John wondered whether she was joking or was really so incredibly punctual that she counted every second. The woman seemed so odd, it could have been either.

Inside, he blinked in surprise. John knew Wortham Court School was fancy from the brochures he'd been sent when they offered him a full scholarship, but the bus made the first-class cabin of a plane look like a farmyard truck. High-tech and luxurious, the seats were wide and black and looked like expensive modern armchairs. Above each of them was an overhead computer screen with information scrolling across. The black carpeting was so soft that even through the soles of his sneakers, it felt like his feet were being gently massaged. Everything was polished and gleaming.

But something nagged at the back of his brain. Apart from the fact that it looked like it had cost a fortune, there was something wrong with the bus. Something John couldn't quite put his finger on.

Behind him, the woman said, "Sixteen seconds."

John sank into an empty seat that swallowed him up in soft comfort. He ran a hand over the surface, not recognizing the marshmallowy material. Frowning slightly, he watched the woman climb the steps. She moved like she was carrying heavy weights and puffed with effort.

"Please strap yourself in for departure," the

woman said loudly before she dropped into the seat across the walkway from John's.

He reached back. The straps, too, were weird, more like a harness than a normal seatbelt. One strap fitted over each shoulder and they clipped together over his chest. With a soft *vipp* sound, they automatically tightened, holding him securely in the seat.

This school must take safety way seriously.

His thoughts were interrupted by a soft chiming sound. Then a voice that John thought must be coming from hidden speakers said, "Stand by for departure."

The bus began to vibrate softly, although there was no noise from the engine.

As John looked out the window, hoping for a last glimpse of his house, it dawned on him what had been bothering him.

"Hey!" he shouted. As the woman turned to

face him, he looked at her in total confusion. "There's no driver. Where's the driver?"

He caught a brief glimpse of her puzzled face, and then the bus began moving.

John's eyes widened as the front of the bus lifted up smoothly until it was pointing straight up at the sky. He gasped as his weight settled into the back of his seat. In front, where he had been able to see the road through the windshield a moment before, clouds now moved slowly across the sky.

"What the —"

The soft chime rang again. "Boosters engaged," said the disembodied voice.

The words in John's mouth turned into a choking noise as, with a slight jolt, the bus leaped upward.

Unable to speak, he jerked his head to the side, just in time to see the roof of a house and the topmost leaves of a tall tree rush past the window next to him.

"Acceleration procedure initiated. Escape velocity in three, two, one —"

There was a terrifying burst of speed. John was pushed back into his seat by an invisible force. It felt like his skin was trying to crawl to the back of his head.

Unable to move, John looked out of the corner of his eye toward the windshield again. The bus plunged into the underside of a cloud.

A heartbeat later, it swept out into clear blue. It was moving faster now, powering higher and higher.

"*Whoa!*" John gasped. Seconds ago he'd been sitting in a bus at the end of his street. Now the "bus" had turned into some sort of aircraft and was rocketing away from the ground at a furious speed. He stared ahead, his mind boggling. He closed his eyes. The view was exactly the same when he opened them again, though the sky ahead was darker now, a deep velvety blue.

Feeling like his brain was being scrambled, John racked his thoughts for a reasonable explanation. Then for an *un*reasonable explanation. *Anything* that made any sense at all.

Another chime. The voice spoke again, sounding ridiculously calm. "We have now left Earth's atmosphere."

John's jaw dropped open as the words sank in. There was nothing outside the Earth's atmosphere.

Nothing but . . .

He couldn't bring himself to even think about what his brain was trying to tell him.

The voice interrupted his gibbering thoughts once more. "Particle drive engaged. Three-quarters light speed and accelerating."

Nothing but . . .

Space.

CHAPTER 2

"*Gah!*" John shouted in confusion. With effort, he turned his head to look out the window. Falling away below, there was now what looked like a map of England, outlined by blue.

He stared wildly at it.

Impossible.

Now England was just a small shape on a blue and green ball, ribboned with white and shining against blackness. To one side, a smaller, silvery ball was slowly moving behind it.

For a second he struggled to understand

what he was seeing. But the part of his brain that wasn't completely panicking gave him the answer: that was Earth, with the moon spinning around it.

I'm in space. Impossible. It's impossible.

The chiming sound came again, followed by the calm voice. "You may remove your safety harness and move around the shuttle."

The force that had pinned him to his seat was gone now. Hearing what sounded like a sigh, John turned his head away from the window. Part of him felt like screaming, part of him wanted to laugh, as he watched the woman who had hurried him onto the bus remove her wig. She let it go and it floated beside her.

The woman's head was bald and almost the same height as her wig. She took a small tube from the breast pocket of her suit and sprayed the contents across the hairless dome of her head and her face. John watched as a layer of makeup dissolved to reveal pale blue skin. She blinked and her eyes changed, becoming black slits, like a snake's, set in bright violet.

Feeling his gaze on her, she turned toward John and gave him a cool smile. "It's a relief to get that off my head," she said. "Stupid thing itches like crazy."

John moved his mouth, but no sound came out.

The woman pressed a button and her harness fell away. Gently drifting upward, she unfolded her long, thin limbs and began spinning in the air as she took off the tweed jacket, revealing a skin-tight silver suit.

Folding the clothes carefully, the woman grabbed the floating wig before it drifted out of reach and, with a flick of her hand, darted upward. She tucked her disguise into an overhead locker and, with another flick, zoomed down until she was resting in her seat again.

Stretching her legs out with another deep sigh, she continued talking. "Of course the gravity on Earth is much too strong for us Elvians. Not good for the joints, you know?"

Still unable to speak, John leaned over and looked back at the rows of seats behind him.

I must be going insane. That's it, I've completely lost it.

The other passengers were as weird as the woman next to him. *No*, he corrected himself: *weirder.*

In the seat immediately behind him was a creature that looked a little like a dolphin with arms and legs. It was wearing a black all-in-one suit, its head covered with a clear helmet filled with bubbling water.

The dolphin's mouth opened and closed. An

electronic-sounding voice from a panel on the front of its suit said, "What are *you* staring at, newbie? Never seen a P'sidion before?"

"Uh . . . no. No, I haven't," John choked, his own voice sounding small and hoarse.

"Well, you're getting a good eyeful now. Didn't anyone ever tell you it's rude to stare?"

John tore his eyes away from the creature, and instantly found himself staring again.

In the row behind the P'sidion was an insect-like being with six spindly legs and huge eyes made up of hundreds of tiny hexagons. Its mouthparts clicked and buzzed, making a girl with jet-black skin across from him laugh. She looked almost human, apart from bright yellow eyes and the two stubby feelers on her forehead.

"I don't believe you, Kritta," she said, giggling at the insect-creature. "You so did *not* go solar flare surfing on Erraticus Six."

Farther back were more strange-looking beings. One looked a little like a frog with orange skin. Another was covered in thick fur. Its long, sharp teeth showed when it laughed.

John's attention was distracted for a moment as a pale yellow ball circled by a shimmering halo passed by the window.

Saturn, his brain told him matter-of-factly.

No. Freaking. Way.

Biting his lip, he watched until the majestic planet slipped out of view, then turned back to look at the other people on the bus.

Not "people." Aliens. They're all aliens.

A few rows back, an alien wearing something that looked like sunglasses, but with four lenses instead of two, settled back in its seat and flipped open a small device. The beat of weird music filled the shuttle. A hologram of a woman with eight arms began dancing above the tiny machine. A girl whose head bristled with metallic spikes leaned forward for a better look.

"Zero-G war!" shouted an alien with bright green eyes and a floor-length tail of purple hair falling from a knot on the top of his head. The alien unclipped his seat belt and sailed through the air toward the seat opposite. The female creature sitting there, who looked as though she was covered in tiny tattoos, spilled her drink in surprise. Blobs of liquid floated past her and splattered into smaller blobs on the window.

Scowling, she threw the empty cup, hitting the purple-haired alien on the forehead and sending him floating off, giggling, in the opposite direction.

"You are such an idiot, Lishtig!" the tattooed girl shouted.

Purple-haired Lishtig crashed into a gray alien with an almost triangular head and spindly limbs. His huge, black eyes blinked in shock and a small mouth opened in what John thought must be a grin.

"Got you!" he shouted, pushing Lishtig away with an enormous heave that sent him hurtling along the length of the bus.

Unclipping his own harness, the gray alien kicked off from his seat and soared into the air. As he passed the row in front, he reached down with one long, three-fingered hand and grabbed a metallic packet from the claw of the alien sitting there.

"Yes!" he shouted. "Galva-coated Dumpod candies. Who wants one?"

"Hey, those are mine, Bareon. Give them back!"

"Come and get them," yelled the gray alien, throwing one of the pieces of candy along the length of the bus and hitting another alien on the head. That head was covered in small tentacles.

"Mine," the tentacled alien said, laughing. A tentacle snapped out and wrapped around the candy, pulling it into the alien's beak-like mouth. "Thanks, Bareon."

By now, the candy's owner was flying along the bus, claws outstretched to snap at Bareon.

Someone started chanting, "Zero-G, Zero-G, Zero-G," as a couple of aliens crashed into each other and began tussling in mid-air.

By now, other aliens were joining in. The shouting of "Zero-G, Zero-G!" became louder and louder, as floating aliens tumbled around the bus in a mass of arms, legs, tentacles, claws, fins — and body parts that John couldn't recognize.

"Not joining in?" asked the P'Sidion in the seat behind John.

"Um . . . I don't know how," John replied, as

the dolphin-like alien kicked away toward the scrum.

It looked back over its shoulder. "It's a Zero-Gravity war," its voice panel shouted over the noise. "Float and fight. That's all there is to it."

Even in his shocked state, John thought Zero-G war looked like a lot of fun. Usually only astronauts got to experience zero gravity. In the pictures he'd seen, he was always amazed that none of them ever looked as though they were really enjoying the experience.

For the first time since the bus left Earth, John smiled. He looked down and was surprised to find that his fingers had already unclipped his safety harness.

John twisted to look behind him. "How do you . . . *whooooa!*" he spluttered, as the movement sent him spinning into the air, feet and hands windmilling as he tried to keep his balance.

"I — I'm flying!" John yelled, as he floated down the aisle in slow somersaults. "Help!"

A hand grabbed his shoulder, steadying him. John looked up into Lishtig's grinning face. "Thanks," he panted. "I've never done this before."

"It's your first time playing Zero-G war? Wow, your planet must be dull."

"Uh, no. My first time in zero gravity."

Lishtig's eyes widened in shock. "You have to be kidding me," he laughed. "Is that why you were floating around like a panicking Scrabbler Beast? It was hilarious."

"Hey, I was just starting to get the hang of it."

"Then don't let me keep you." The purple-haired alien pushed John toward the back of the shuttle with a flick of his wrist.

Laughing, John cartwheeled through the

air. He was completely out of control, but flying along the bus was an incredible feeling. He touched a passing seat, managing to stop himself from tumbling.

This must be how superheroes feel, he thought, as he sailed down the aisle.

The next moment, he crashed headlong into Bareon, who, in turn, crashed into the aliens sitting in the back row.

"Ms. Vartexia, can't you keep the first years under control?" yelled the girl with metallic spikes on her head. "We're trying to watch *Black Hole Hospital* and they're *ruining* it."

Bareon ignored her and shouted, "I'll get you for that, Lishtig!" Bracing his feet against a window, he heaved John back toward the front of the shuttle.

"*Oh nooooo!*" John yelled through his laughter, clawing at the air as he smashed into the P'Sidion, who thrust him off down the aisle again.

Just as his head was about to connect with the windshield, a hand caught his ankle. Expertly, Ms. Vartexia twisted him away and sent him flying back into his seat.

"Settle down now!" shouted the blue-skinned woman. She turned toward the back of the bus and clapped her hands. "If you can't behave like advanced beings, then I shall turn the gravity on."

"Aww, Ms. Vartexia!" shouted Lishtig. "We're only having fun. Shuttle flights are *so* boring."

"That's *enough*, Lishtig," Ms. Vartexia replied sternly. "Everyone back to their seats *now*. We'll be docking in just under four minutes, so try to be sensible until then."

Grumbling, the aliens broke away and floated back to their seats.

As Ms. Vartexia sat back down, John remembered that he was supposed to be on a bus to boarding school. "Um, excuse me. Where are we going?" he blurted.

The Elvian gave him a sharp glance. "We're on our way to school, of course," she said.

"Um . . . I'm supposed to be going to Wortham Court School. We're not going to the Wortham Court School, are we?"

If the last question had been ridiculous, this one was clearly utterly bonkers.

John blushed as the alien woman looked at him again with an expression that asked, *Are you really that stupid?*

She blinked her violet eyes at him and said, "Ah ha ha. I'm sure that is extremely amusing to your species. We Elvians do not, however, have a sense of humor. As you know perfectly well, we are going to Hyperspace High. If you look out the viewing window, you can see the ship now."

John turned his head. His eyes widened in disbelief. Once again, he felt like his brain was melting.

Even at a distance, he could tell the spaceship was vast. Its shape looked like a gigantic ocean liner with a million windows twinkling against sweeping curves of white. A short "neck" stretched forward from the main body of the ship. It ended in a smaller "head" that blazed with lights. On either side were two wings, slightly curved, which gave the impression of both power and speed. Behind the main part of the body, the ship tapered into a sleek tail.

John stared as it looked bigger and bigger through the window. The spaceship was easily the size of a small city.

"Hyperspace High," said Ms. Vartexia.

"It's impressive the first time you see it, isn't it?" Without waiting for a reply, she continued. "The main bridge is the ring of lights you can see at the front and at the other end is the very latest Galaxy-Star Hyperspatial Drive. The wings contain sensors, force-field generators, hanger decks for shuttles and smaller ships while the main body houses the school. Sixty-four levels of classrooms, lecture halls, athletic fields, dormitories, restaurants, laboratories, and technology workshops."

She paused for a moment, then finished with quiet pride, "It's the finest school in the universe."

CHAPTER 3

"It's incredible," John whispered. "The most amazing thing I've ever seen."

In fact, the word *amazing* didn't do it justice. Hyperspace High made *Star Trek*'s *USS Enterprise* look like a plastic toy spaceship in comparison. John had thought that Wortham Court School looked impressive in its shiny brochure — but this school was in a league of its own.

The chiming sounded again, and the voice said, "Please take your seats for docking."

John slumped back into the seat. It crossed his

mind again that he might have gone insane, but he didn't *feel* crazy. Apart from the whole being-in-space thing, he felt pretty normal. Under his breath he muttered, "My name is John Riley, I live at 112 Laurel Street. I like video games. I have never — not once — worn my pants on my head. I am definitely not insane."

That left one possibility. This was *real*. He was on a shuttle that was now docking at a vast spaceship on the outer edges of the solar system. His face opened into a huge grin.

Wow.

As the shuttle approached, a huge door on the side of the spaceship slid open.

The shuttle landed with a light jolt. Gravity returned.

Instantly, the rest of the passengers began babbling.

"Yay, we're here. I'm off first."

"Out of my way, Voolon. I want to get the best bed pod in the dormitory."

"Do you think Ska's Café has Fettid Jax Fruit this year?"

"That's *my* bag, Esterlin."

Ms. Vartexia got to her feet. "Please exit the shuttle in a calm and orderly manner and form a line at Exit Port Beta, where an Examiner will register you," she ordered, as the door slid open with a faint hiss.

None of the aliens aboard seemed to be paying any attention. They pushed past her, shouting and laughing, as they crammed through the door.

She sighed and waited until the crowd had passed before reaching up to take her wig and tweed suit from the locker. Catching sight of John, still in his seat, she said sharply, "Please join your fellow students in the line at Exit Port

Beta." She nodded toward the door. "Examiners do not like to be kept waiting."

John took a deep breath. "Look," he said slowly and clearly. "This is *waaay* amazing and everything but, really, I'm supposed to be on a bus to Wortham Court School —"

"In Dar Bee Shur, wherever that is. Yes. So you said. And as I told *you*, Elvians are not known for their sense of humor. Please join your fellow students in the line at Exit Port Beta."

"But —"

"I have already made one note, of your late arrival. Please leave the shuttle before I make another."

Seeing that the alien woman wasn't going to listen, John unclipped his seat belt, grabbed his backpack, and climbed down the steps.

He found himself in a vast, white space. The shuttle had landed at the end of a row of similar craft. They all looked like the gleaming silver bus he had boarded earlier.

"Over there."

His eyes followed her pointing finger to where a line had formed. "Is there anyone else I can talk to?" he asked as he hiked the backpack up onto his shoulder and started walking.

"If you continue this behavior, you will very soon find yourself talking to the headmaster."

"Can't I speak to him now?"

"Enough! Get in the line."

Not knowing what might happen if he made the tall, blue alien angry, John joined the others. The other aliens glanced at him curiously.

John peered around them. At the front of the line was an egg-shaped robot with a round head that blinked a red light as it scanned the new arrivals.

The Examiner, John thought. It was as white

as the ship itself and floated above the floor as though weightless.

Light flickered over the alien boy with the purple hair. "Lishtig ar Steero," said an electronic, droning voice. "Pass."

The boy whooped and ran off down the hallway, shouting "First bed pod is *mine!*"

"Kritta Askin-Tarsos," said the Examiner. "Pass."

John hopped from one foot to the other nervously as he waited his turn.

Gradually the line shrank, until only the black girl with yellow eyes and feelers stood in front of John.

"Queelin Temerate of Bo Four. Pass."

John stepped forward nervously. The red light scanned his feet and started moving up his body.

John blinked as it passed over his eyes.

A harsh siren began wailing.

"No identification match. Intruder at Exit Port Beta."

A small door hissed open farther down the hallway. John saw another Examiner shoot down the corridor toward him. Lights flashed on its blank face and, at once, a shimmering green haze wrapped itself around John. He felt his feet leave the floor.

Fighting panic, he tried to look for the Elvian woman, but he couldn't move his head.

"Force field activated. Intruder neutralized," the new Examiner said tonelessly. "Access the secondary DNA database."

Once more a red light swept over John.

There was a short pause, then the first Examiner said, "Human. Male. Native to a sub-B primitive planet called Earth."

The new Examiner turned slightly toward

John. "State your name and purpose," it said in its cold, electronic voice.

John felt a slight tingling sensation around his head and found that he could move it again. "John . . . uh . . . Riley," he said. "I'm just trying to get to school. Wortham Court School."

From the corner of his eye, John saw Ms. Vartexia step forward. "He's been saying that since we picked him up," she said. "I thought he was trying to be funny."

"There's obviously been a mistake," John said quickly. "But if you just take me back, I swear I won't say any —"

"Unauthorized intruder. Procedure: expulsion," the robot continued, ignoring him.

"That seems —" Ms. Vartexia began.

"Affirmative," the first Examiner interrupted. "Security breach confirmed. Expulsion code initiated. Proceed to Airlock Seventeen."

"Fine. Go ahead and expel me," John said, shrugging. But suddenly a terrible thought crossed his mind.

"Wait! Hang on a second!" John heard himself shouting. He struggled, but could not get free of the force field that held him in place. "What do you mean by *expulsion*?"

"Oh dear. I can't help feeling that this is partly my fault, John Uh Riley," said Ms. Vartexia with a sigh. "Sorry."

"W-what? Why are you s-sorry?" John stammered.

The green force field shimmered around him. As the Examiner moved forward, John floated backward into the shuttle hangar. Exit Port Beta hissed closed. Ms. Vartexia waved goodbye.

"Where are you taking me?" John yelled.

The robot did not reply.

Another door opened. John dropped to the floor as it closed behind him.

Free of the force field, he beat his fists against a window, shouting after the Examiner as it skimmed away.

"Airlock Seventeen. Expulsion Code eight five six three. Decompression in five seconds," said a deeper electronic voice.

John looked over his shoulder. Behind him was a heavy doorway. Through a small window he could see stars beyond.

"Four."

With growing horror, he realized that the door was going to open. Within seconds he would be expelled into space.

"Three."

Frozen with fear, he whispered, "No," staring wide-eyed at the door.

"Two."

It began to hiss.

"One."

CHAPTER 4

John clenched his fists. His knees trembled; his heart thudded against his ribs. This was it: he was going to die.

In a second he would be thrown into space. John remembered learning at school that nothing could live in that cold vacuum. After a few minutes he'd be frozen solid, spinning through the black depths forever. Thoughts of his mom and dad chased across his mind. They would never know what happened to him. He squeezed his eyes shut, dreading the sound of the airlock opening and the rush of air that would suck him out.

But nothing happened.

A second passed. It felt like an eternity.

"Emergency override activated," said the deep electronic voice.

John opened a fearful eye just in time to see a ball of brightly flashing light pass through the door as if it weren't there. His other eye opened in shock.

For a moment, the ball hung in mid-air, then suddenly, it expanded. John watched, open-mouthed, as the glittering ball formed into the solid figure of a man. He was of human average height and almost human-looking, aside from the fact that his skin was still faintly glowing. Completely bald, he looked old, but somehow young at the same time.

It was his eyes, John realized. His purple eyes twinkled as if he were enjoying a private joke.

Trembling, John said, "What . . . I mean, *who* are you?"

The old man tilted his head to one side and regarded John quietly for a moment. Then, with a slight smile, he said, "I am Lorem, the headmaster of Hyperspace High."

"If you're the headmaster, then I . . . I think . . . that is, I'd like to make a complaint." John paused, then added, "Sir."

The strangely glowing headmaster nodded as if he had been expecting just that. But before John could continue, Lorem held up one finger and said, "Excuse me one moment."

Looking into Lorem's face, John had to obey. There was laughter in the headmaster's sparkling eyes, but also a quiet authority that couldn't be ignored. John closed his mouth.

Lorem turned toward the door. The two Examiners and Ms. Vartexia had arrived. "What is going on here?" Lorem asked. His voice sounded perfectly polite, but it held a trace of steel. John guessed that the headmaster was annoyed.

"School rule six four two eight B forbids unauthorized personnel on the ship. Procedure: expulsion," one of the Examiners droned.

"More like being thrown out into space to die," John muttered.

The Examiners ignored him. The second said, "It is male. Human. A minor, undeveloped species . . ."

"Hey, humans aren't undeveloped —" John began.

"School rule 8675C: contradicting Examiners is forbidden. Procedure —"

"Enough," said Lorem. John and the

Examiner both fell silent. Turning back to John, the headmaster raised an eyebrow. "You mentioned a complaint."

John took a deep breath. "Yes, well, these things tried to kill me. I didn't ask to be here. I tried to tell Ms. . . . um, Ms. Vartexia . . . but she wouldn't listen to me."

"I'm embarrassed to say that he's telling the truth, Headmaster," Ms. Vartexia admitted. "I was told to expect a Martian prince who would be disguised as a human and we were running a little late for the departure window." She held her hands up and said apologetically, "I thought he was trying to joke with me. You know what Martians are like." She stopped for a moment, then said, "I really am most dreadfully sorry. He says his name is John Uh Riley, if that's any help."

Lorem gave her a stern look. "So, Prince

Clo-Ra-Ta has been left behind and we have, instead, taken an Earthling called John Uh Riley, breaking several galactic laws about revealing advanced technology to primitive species. The Martian government will not be happy. The Galactic Council will not be happy. Come to think of it, *I* am not happy."

"It's just *John Riley*, actually," John interrupted. "No 'Uh.' And I'm sorry, but are you saying there are *Martians*, from *Mars*, on Earth?"

The headmaster turned back to him. "Don't worry. Your planet isn't being invaded. Martians just like taking vacations there."

"The royal family is staying in the bed and breakfast at 114 Laurel Street, according to my records," said Ms. Vartexia, glancing once again at her thin screen. She seemed nervous. John guessed she was trying to be extra helpful after making such a huge mistake. "Strange place for a vacation, if you ask me, but Martians can be a little odd."

"But 114 Laurel Street is next door to my house!" John spluttered. He remembered the family that had arrived there at the beginning of summer. They *had* been weird. Every time he'd seen them, the parents' clothes had been badly matched and worn back-to-front or inside-out. He'd once spoken to their son. The skinny, lonely-looking boy had been holding an umbrella on a clear summer afternoon and had asked in a weird accent why John's skateboard didn't fly.

"They were *Martians*?" John blurted. "Actual Martians? I thought they'd be, you know, little green men or something. I didn't think they'd carry umbrellas everywhere."

"Without the human disguise, Martians are,

in fact, a very pleasing shade of orange," Lorem explained. "And Earth is closer to the sun than Mars. The sunlight on your planet is too strong for them, so they protect themselves from it with portable shade devices. I believe humans use these *um-brel-ahs*, as you call them, to prevent water falling from the sky from soaking their clothing."

"Wow, I've met a Martian prince," John whispered. "No one will ever believe me when I get back. . . ." He looked at Lorem questioningly. "I *am* going back, aren't I? You're not going to toss me out the airlock, right?"

"No. It appears a genuine mistake has been made. You have my apologies for that, and for the Examiners' hasty and regrettable actions. They should *not* have tried to expel you." Lorem shot the two robots a glance. "I'm sure there are rules being broken elsewhere," he finished.

"Rule breaking will result in disciplinary procedures," the Examiners announced together. Then, to John's relief, they turned and floated away.

"Can I go home now?" John asked. "I don't know how I'm going to explain where I've been, but if you drop me off where you found me, I can still get Mom to drive me to school. I shouldn't be too late."

Lorem met his gaze. John got the feeling he was looking into eyes that had seen things he couldn't even begin to understand. "I'm afraid it will be a while before you get back to Earth," the headmaster said sorrowfully. He raised a finger again as John started to protest. "Hyperspace High is a vast vessel moving at many, many times the speed of light. It takes six weeks to make a complete circuit of the galaxy. We cannot simply stop and turn around. It would involve colossal energies and our schedule would be thrown off completely."

"What about the shuttles? Couldn't one of them take me?"

"You don't understand how fast this ship is," Lorem replied. "We have already passed the star your scientists call *Epsilon Eridani*, which is more than ten light-years, or six *trillion* miles, from your sun. A shuttle would take months to cover that distance."

John gulped. "So . . . what do I do now, then?"

"We will pass your solar system again at the end of this semester. Until then, you will have to stay on board."

"But when I don't show up at school, my parents will be worried sick. The police will start looking for me."

The headmaster smiled at him. "This ship

is equipped with quite astonishing technology," he said quietly. "It can easily patch into Earth's communication systems. You will be able to speak to your parents on the telephone or send emails so they think you have arrived at school safely. And I can tell the headmaster of Wortham Court School that you have been taken suddenly ill with some human sickness that will take several weeks to clear up. Ms. Vartexia, perhaps you could make yourself useful and suggest a suitable human disease."

The thin Elvian woman tapped her screen a few times. "It says here that humans often take weeks to recover from something called 'measles.'"

"There we are. Measles it is," said the headmaster. "Now, our last problem is what to do with you. You're a little young to be a teacher, so I think we'll have to enroll you as a temporary student. The first years are starting their second term, but I'm sure you'll soon catch up."

John thought for a moment. Though he'd never been a great fan of school, except for math classes, he guessed that space school — a school in actual *space* — would be much, *much* cooler than Wortham Court. For a start, he wanted another try at Zero-G war. And, after all, it would only be for a few weeks.

He grinned. Nodded. "Yeah, that sounds okay."

Lorem clapped his hands together. "*Excellent,*" he said. "Then that is one problem solved. Ms. Vartexia, to which dormitory was Prince Clo-Ra-Ta assigned?"

She tapped her screen again. "Dormitory sixteen, room twelve."

Something seemed to amuse the headmaster. "Of course," he said, chuckling. "That's perfect.

Well, Clo-Ra-Ta won't be needing it, so if you'd like to come with me, young human, we'll get you settled in. Ms. Vartexia, I'm sure you would like to rest after your eventful trip. Perhaps you'd be so kind as to join me in my office in, say, three hours?"

John followed the glowing headmaster out of the airlock, wondering if the Martian prince had also boarded the wrong bus and was now on his way to Wortham Court. He pictured the lonely young Martian with his weird umbrella and hoped not.

But if he did get on the wrong bus, at least there's no danger of him being pushed out of an airlock, he told himself.

Now that his life was out of danger, John looked around eagerly. Everywhere was white and spotless. "This is the hangar deck," Lorem said over his shoulder. "Not terribly interesting, but we'll have someone give you a full tour of the ship later. Down here, please."

John followed the headmaster along an empty hallway, a hundred questions bubbling up in his mind. "She's not in trouble, is she?" he asked first. "It was an honest mistake, really."

"Ms. Vartexia? Oh, no. The Martians will grumble, but they are an extremely forgiving people. The prince is going to be more than happy with an unexpected extra vacation, though he missed last term, too. A diplomatic mission to Kantaros with his parents, I believe. We may have to put him back a year . . . but I'm getting off the point. The Galactic Council is not going to care very much. You'll tell a few people the truth when you get back to Earth, but no one will believe you. Still, I *am* going to ask Ms. Vartexia to be a little more careful in the future. She won't make that mistake again."

John frowned. The way Lorem spoke, it sounded as if he already knew what was going to happen. The thought was quickly pushed aside by another question. "Um, if everyone here is an alien, why do you all speak English so well?"

Lorem looked back at him again, an eyebrow arched as if to say, *You humans really are primitive aren't you?*, but he answered politely. "The only person aboard this ship speaking English is *you*. The ship's computer automatically translates all known languages into whichever one you understand best. It's all to do with sound waves. Simple, really. Ah, here we are."

They had arrived at the end of a hallway. Lorem touched his hand to the wall and a door slid back. John joined him in what he guessed was an elevator. "Dormitory sixteen," said Lorem.

At once, the elevator slid away smoothly in

a diagonal direction. John opened his mouth to ask another question, but the headmaster was already speaking.

"By the way," he said. "Please don't use the word *alien* here. That word means something that doesn't belong. No one is an alien on Hyperspace High. We all belong here."

"Sorry," said John. "I guess there's a lot I'll have to get used to."

Lorem looked at him kindly. "Oh, yes," he said. "But don't worry, you're going to be just fine."

The elevator stopped. "Dormitory sixteen," said its electronic voice.

As the door slid open, John saw a wide, richly carpeted room. The lights were dimmer here and the air was filled with a soothing smell that was new to John's nose. In the middle of the room was a sculpture that looked as though it had been carved from a huge diamond. Lights shining onto it made hundreds of small rainbows. Scattered about were comfortable-looking sofas on which a few students sat, chatting.

Each side of the room was lined with doorways. Lorem quickly walked over to one and held up a hand. The door made a soft chiming sound. A moment later, it slid open.

John took a step back. Despite all the strange things he'd seen, he couldn't stop himself from gasping in shock.

Standing in the doorway was a massive figure straight out of a nightmare. Easily eight feet tall and heavily muscled, its skin was bright green and its eyes deep red. Over its shoulders, John could see black wings folded on its back.

A demon. It's a real, live demon.

For the second time that day, John felt his heart thudding against his chest in terror.

The creature's mouth opened, revealing wickedly sharp fangs. With a rustle of leathery wings, the demon fixed him with its crimson gaze and advanced toward him menacingly.

CHAPTER 5

John fought down an urge to turn and run, but Lorem put a reassuring hand on his arm as if he knew exactly what John was feeling.

"John Riley," Lorem said, "I'd like to introduce you to your new roommate. Kaal is from the planet Derril. The two of you are going to be great friends."

"Hello, Headmaster. What a pleasant surprise."

John was amazed. The creature's voice was soft, and the smile that spread across its face looked shy. It took a step back and said, "Please come in."

"Thank you, but I must speak to the Martian government, so I'll leave you to get to know each other. Kaal, perhaps you could give John Riley a tour of the ship when he's unpacked." Lorem's hand dropped away from John's arm. For a moment he paused, then added, "And, by the way, fighting with Mordant Talliver would probably *not* be a good idea. Just some friendly advice. Take it or leave it."

"Wha—" John began, but it was too late to question the headmaster. In a blink, Lorem's body dissolved into a ball of glowing light that disappeared through the far wall.

Confused enough to forget how nervous the huge green Derrilian made him, John said, "What on Earth was he talking about?"

Kaal looked down at him, puzzled, and

asked, "What do you mean? Don't you know about Lorem?"

"Um, no. I'm not really supposed to be here. I'd never heard of Lorem or Hyperspace High until half an hour ago."

"Well, he can see the future. The past, too. So when he says we're going to be great friends, he's probably right." Kaal raised a hand, stopped, and then said shyly, "How do your people greet each other?"

"We shake hands, usually."

Kaal stretched out a hand. "Like this?"

"Yes," said John, taking Kaal's enormous, six-fingered hand in his own and shaking it. "And . . . um . . . how about your people?"

"Oh, we bite each other's faces," replied Kaal, bending over him. With a grin, he revealed his sharp white teeth again.

"Aaargh," John choked.

"Joking. I'm just joking! On Derril we touch each other on the shoulder and wish them good flight. Like this." Kaal gently put his hand on John's shoulder and said, "Wide skies, John Riley. Come in and put your bag down."

John grinned back at his roommate, Lorem's strange warning quickly forgotten. He already liked Kaal. "You can call me John," he said, hitching his backpack up his shoulder and following the green alien into the room.

"Wow!" he said.

The far wall was a floor-to-ceiling window that showed the full glory of space. Outside, a great cloud of swirling dust and newborn stars, which John knew was called a nebula — swept past. John tore his eyes away from the view with difficulty and looked around.

Room twelve looked like it belonged in a five-star hotel. There were two enormous, soft sofas with a low table between them and what John guessed must be a workstation with comfortable-looking chairs and two thin screens. One wall had a beautifully detailed picture of the ship. At each end of the room were what looked like smaller rooms.

"I hope you don't mind, but I've already chosen that one," said Kaal apologetically, pointing. John peered closer and realized that the smaller rooms were, in fact, giant, enclosed beds.

"You have everything you need in there," Kaal continued. "Hologram projector, an entertainment ThinScreen, food and drink portals, communications, and access to the main computer. And if you get sick of looking at me, just touch here."

He pressed a finger against a panel and a screen instantly hissed down, cutting the bed off from the main room. "You might want to use that anyway. I snore."

"It's amazing," John whispered.

"Bathroom's in here," Kaal said, touching another panel. Another door slid open, revealing another large room that contained what looked like a small swimming pool. Seeing John's astonished face, he added, "They have to make everything big because some of us at Hyperspace High are pretty huge compared to the rest of you. There's an automatic cleaning system, too, if you don't like taking baths."

John dropped his backpack on the free bed. "If this is the *bedroom*, what's the rest of the ship like?" he asked.

"Pretty cool. Want to see?"

"Are you kidding? Let's go."

"Don't you want to unpack?" Kaal asked.

"I'll do it later. Besides, I don't have much.

All my luggage went to a different school." A sudden realization hit John. He looked down at what he was wearing. "Guess I'd better get used to wearing these clothes."

"Why? We can get you some more. There's other stuff you'll need, too."

John fished in his pocket and pulled out the twenty-dollar bill his father had slipped in earlier. "I'm not going to be able to afford much," he said. "Maybe a few pairs of socks."

Kaal looked down at him, confused. "The school provides everything you need," he said. "No one *pays* for anything."

John shook his head in disbelief. *All of these expensive-looking supplies are free?*

A few minutes later, they left their room and strolled along a wide, softly lit corridor. "So you really don't know anything about Hyperspace High at all?"

"Nothing at all," John confirmed. "I was going to a normal boarding school on Earth but got on the wrong bus."

"That's strange," Kaal said thoughtfully. "Lorem should have known that was going to happen. Maybe it wasn't really a mistake. . . ."

But before John could ask Kaal what he meant by it not being a mistake, the Derrilian stopped at a large, transparent door and changed the subject. "This is the astronomy holo-lab."

John peered through the glass. Inside, a small alien with smooth white skin and six dark eyes was standing in the center of the room. Around it whirled a complicated system of twin suns and planets.

John watched as the alien touched a screen. Instantly, one of the planets grew and revolved in front of the white being. Another touch and the planet became even bigger. John could see seas, rivers, and mountain ranges crossing its continents.

Kaal tutted. "Typical. Term hasn't even started and Raytanna's already studying."

"Looks *way* more interesting than the classrooms I'm used to," said John.

"Come on, there's plenty more to see and classes don't start for a while."

As they continued down the corridor, Kaal made a complex hand gesture at a passing figure wearing a thick, hooded robe. It stopped and bowed deeply. Kaal bowed back. After a second, John followed his example.

The hooded figure bowed a little deeper, then continued on its way. Kaal whispered, "That's Mang. He doesn't say much, but when he speaks it's worth listening to him."

"You were saying something about Hyperspace High," John reminded him.

"Oh yeah, sorry." Kaal took a deep breath and continued in a voice that sounded like he was reading from a brochure. "Hyperspace High was founded by the scholars of Kerallin almost ten thousand years ago."

"This ship doesn't look that old."

"It's not. The school's old but it moves to a new ship every so often. Last time was only a couple of years ago."

"So who are these scholars of Kera— what?"

"Kerallin. Well, few people ever see them, but they're crazy about learning and founded the school as a gift to the universe. Its mission is to give one being from each solar system the best education available anywhere. So far it's produced one hundred and seventy planetary presidents, four hundred and twenty-one Ogloon Prize-winning scientists, countless important artists, explorers and — unfortunately — four intergalactic warlords, but there's always a few who spoil it for everyone else. Hey, this is the technology workshop."

John peered through a set of double doors to see a long hall filled with workbenches and lined with neat lockers. On display were a variety of devices, some of which were moving slowly. "What are they?" he asked.

"Last year's best technology projects. Oh, wow!"

"What?"

"Amazing! Look at Master Tronic," replied Kaal, pointing.

A large jumble of metal was moving at the end of the room. As it unfolded, John realized that it was a hulking robot. Its body was made of cables and big metal plates. A thin band of glowing red flashed across a grinning metal skull.

"What is *that*?" John whispered. "It looks dangerous."

"It's just Master Tronic," said Kaal with a laugh. "Every semester he makes himself a new body to demonstrate what we'll be learning. Last semester we were doing bio-technology, so he made a flesh body, but it looks like we'll be moving on to robotics. Cool!"

John stared at the huge robot, but Kaal was already dragging him away.

"Come on, there's so much to see. Where was I? Oh yeah, so all the students at Hyperspace High are chosen for a reason, though most of the time no one's quite sure what that reason *is*. The scholars of Kerallin are a secretive bunch. But it's a big honor to be chosen. Oh, this is the virtual-reality lecture hall."

For the next hour, Kaal led John around the ship until his head spun and his legs ached from the effort of keeping up with the tall Derrilian. He saw classrooms with holographic teachers, laboratories that couldn't be entered without protective clothing, and gyms where students were practicing games he couldn't begin to understand.

"Okay, last stop is the Center," Kaal said finally. "You're going to *love* it. And we can pick up some new stuff for you there."

"Center," said the voice of the elevator as the door slid open.

John followed Kaal out and found himself gasping for what felt like the thousandth time that day. *Will I ever get used to this?* he thought, trying to take in the sight before him.

They were standing on a balcony in a space like a football stadium. Above was a vast, clear dome through which John could see stars. Below, where the field should have been, was a small forest. Tall trees, of types and colors John had never seen, stretched up toward the dome above. In the middle was a small, sparkling lake, in which students were splashing around. Among the trees were tables where brightly colored beings sat, eating and drinking. Around the edges rose rings of balconies. More aliens — *students*, John corrected himself — were walking around, going in and out of what looked like shops and cafés.

"Awesome, huh?" said Kaal. "This is the Center. It's where everyone meets up. Let's get something to drink, and then we'll grab what you need. Ska's Café is the cool place to hang out right now. It's this way."

Staring ahead, John followed him. Beings of every shape passed by; some on two legs, some on four or six, some floating in mid-air. The beings were every color of the rainbow, and no two were alike. Smooth faces and faces as gnarled as tree roots turned curiously toward him. Other students were covered in technological devices that looked like parts of their bodies.

Every shop they passed was different, too. There was nothing John recognized in any of the window displays. He tried to stop and take a closer look, but Kaal's hand on his shoulder steered him firmly through the crowd.

Inside Ska's Café, groups of students were laughing over tall glasses of bright liquids. The black walls were covered with designs in glowing colors, and the café was filled with a high-pitched wailing sound.

Kaal led John to what looked like a row of microwave ovens along one wall. "Hi," Kaal said. "I'll have a starberry smoothie, and my friend will have a . . . um . . . John, what do you want?"

"Orange juice, please," replied John, wondering who Kaal was talking to.

"*Or-an-jooz?*" said a dry voice. "What planet is that from?"

"Earth," said John, looking around in confusion.

"Earth. Interesting planet, noted for its music." Immediately, the high-pitched wailing sound stopped. John couldn't believe his ears as the sound was replaced with a popular song he'd downloaded the day before. He stared around wildly.

"Drinks are ready," the voice said.

"Thank you . . . and thanks for the music," John said, still looking around.

There was a slight pause. "You're welcome," said the voice quietly. "No one's ever thanked me before."

Before John could reply, Kaal nudged him

and handed him a tall glass of orange juice he'd taken from one of the microwave-type machines.

"Ship's computer," Kaal said, seeing John's questioning face. "Empty table over at the back," he continued, peering over the crowd. "Quick, before someone else takes it."

Sipping his juice, which tasted as if it had been freshly squeezed, John stayed close to the Derrilian as he pushed toward the back of the café.

"Hey, Lishtig," Kaal said, stopping. "Good to see you. This is John Riley. New student."

"We met on the shuttle," said the purple-haired boy. "You're the Martian prince, right?"

"Um, no. There was kind of a mix-up. I'm from Earth."

"I wondered why you hadn't taken off your disguise."

"And this is Gobi-san-Art," Kaal cut in, indicating a creature that looked as if it had been carved from rock. "Gobi, meet John Riley."

"A pleasure to meet you, John Riley," said the being, with a voice that crunched like gravel.

"And this," the Derrilian said, "is Emmie Tarz. Emmie, John Riley. New student."

John's heart leaped as he looked down. Sitting at a table was the most beautiful girl he had ever seen. Her face was almost human — with navy-blue eyes, an upturned nose, and a wide mouth — and her faintly golden skin looked as soft as a peach.

"Welcome aboard," said Emmie, her voice light and musical. John's knees almost gave way as she swept back a mass of shining silvery hair and tucked it behind one of her slightly pointed ears. "Hey, are you okay? Your skin changed color."

Realizing that he was blushing just made John feel even more awkward. "Um, yeah, I'm fine. Uh . . . good . . . good to — yeah, you know."

"And hello to you, too," Emmie replied with a wide smile.

"Come on, John, we're going to lose that table," said Kaal, pulling him away.

Turning away from Emmie, John muttered to himself, "Nice work, Riley. Very cool." He stepped forward and felt something squelch beneath his foot.

"Ow! Watch where you put your feet, you clumsy primitive."

John whirled around to see a figure rising from a nearby seat. Yellow eyes glared at him poisonously. The boy glaring at him was about the same size and shape as John, with two arms and two legs, but he had a great mane of black hair and two black, octopus-like tentacles growing from his ribcage. A small metallic ball was hovering behind him, a gleaming arm extended to brush microscopic specks of dust from his shoulder.

With a sinking feeling, John looked down. He'd stepped on one of the boy's sucker-covered tentacles.

"Are people on your world blind?" the boy spat.

"Perhaps it should be treated with kindness, young Master Talliver," the metallic ball chimed in, its voice snooty. "One must make allowances for these barely evolved species."

"Shut up, G-Vez. I was talking to the primitive," the boy snapped.

John stepped back in surprise. "I'm really sorry," he said. "Totally my fault, I should have been looking —"

"Don't apologize. Mordant was trying to trip you. I saw him."

Emmie Tarz was standing behind him, looking furiously at the black-haired boy. "Nice way to welcome a new student, Mordant," she finished.

"A *student*?" said the hovering ball in a sniffy tone. "It seems standards are falling at Hyperspace High."

"I said *shut up*, G-Vez," Mordant hissed.

"Just as you say, Master Talliver."

The metallic ball retracted its arm and hovered in silence. Mordant turned back to glare at Emmie. "So, it's Tarz to the rescue," he sneered. "The school's most stupid student: Emmie Tarz from planet Stupido."

Emmie's mouth dropped open in shock.

"Surprised the Examiners let you back in this term, Tarz," Mordant continued. "If I were them, I'd dump you in space. Hyperspace High's supposed to have high standards."

"I'd apologize to her right now if I were you, Mordant," growled Kaal. The Derrilian stepped forward, towering over Mordant. Strong muscles shifted beneath his green skin.

"Apologize for what?" Mordant snapped back. "Telling the truth? She's as dumb as a Gullian Plankfish. Everyone knows it."

Kaal's fist lashed out, catching Mordant on the chin. The black-haired boy stumbled backward, knocking over a table and sending drinks flying. Brightly colored liquid splattered onto the floor.

With a sudden shock, John remembered the headmaster's warning about fighting with Mordant Talliver. "Don't do it, Kaal!" he shouted. "Lorem said it wasn't a good idea."

Too late. There was no stopping the fight.

Mordant's tentacles snaked out and wrapped themselves around Kaal's arms, holding him still. He stepped forward and landed a punch in Kaal's stomach.

Roaring, the Derrilian tore the tentacles away and threw himself forward, his wings unfurling and beating in fury.

"Stop it! Stop it!" yelled Emmie Tarz, as Kaal began pummeling Mordant.

"Rule one eight four five A: Physical combat is not permitted on Hyperspace High."

John looked up to see one of the egg-shaped Examiners glide through the doorway. In a flicker of green light, Kaal and Mordant were thrown apart and held still by the Examiner's force fields. "Lorem was right," Kaal groaned. "We're in trouble now."

"Report," said the Examiner in its emotionless electronic voice.

Before Kaal could open his mouth, Mordant quickly said, "It was him. He attacked me for no reason."

"Indeed, the Derrilian began the duel. Master Talliver was simply defending himself," said the hovering G-Vez, sounding bored.

"That's not true," said Emmie. "Mordant tried to trip up the new student and insulted me. Kaal lost his temper, but he was provoked."

"That's right," said John. "We didn't start any trouble."

"They're lying!" yelled Mordant. "Don't believe a word —"

In another flicker of green light, he was silenced.

"A most unfortunate misunderstanding, but young Master Talliver is quite innocent —"

The metal ball was silenced, too.

"Verifying," droned the Examiner. It was

silent for a second, then continued, "The reports from Emmie Tarz and John Riley are accurate. Discipline as follows: Kaal, report to detention room three when classes terminate. Mordant Talliver, report to the headmaster's office immediately." The Examiner's green lights snapped off.

Kaal stood up, crossing his arms over his chest. "You should know by now that you can't lie to an Examiner, Mordant," he said quietly.

"Silence," said the Examiner. "Mordant Talliver, report to the headmaster's office immediately."

Saying nothing, but shooting a look of pure hatred at Kaal, Emmie, and John, Mordant turned and walked quickly out of the café, followed by the metal ball. The Examiner floated after them.

The room fell silent.

John pushed his blond hair out of his eyes and looked at Kaal.

"The Examiners are in charge of discipline," his roommate explained. "They take it really seriously. You do *not* want to mess with them."

"Who *was* the idiot with the tentacles and the freaky ball thing?" John asked.

"Just because his father's got loads of money, Mordant Talliver thinks he's the greatest thing since hyperspace technology. And the ball is G-Vez — a Serve-U-Droid. They're sort of a cross between a pet and a servant; really expensive and completely loyal to their owners. Most people think they're a little weird."

"No kidding —" John was interrupted by a loud chime.

"Oh no, it's later than I thought," Kaal said. "Classes start in five minutes and we've got to get to the hangar deck. We'll never make it."

He clutched his head. "First day of term and I'm gonna get *two* detentions. Plus, extra work. Sergeant Jegger *hates* lateness."

"Who is Sergeant Jegger?"

"No time for questions. Just run!"

CHAPTER 6

John and Kaal were already sprinting when a voice behind them shouted, "Hey, wait for me!" Glancing over his shoulder, John saw Emmie pushing her way through the crowd. "I've got the same class," she said, panting as she ran up beside him. "Come on."

The three sprinted into an elevator and hit the far wall in a jumble. "Hangar deck C!" yelled Kaal. "As fast as possible."

The elevator plunged downward at heart-stopping speed. After a few seconds it lurched sideways, flinging them in a different direction. "Whoa, not *quite* so fast," said Kaal, catching Emmie's slim figure just before her head slammed against the wall. The elevator slowed obediently and a few moments later the door slid open.

"Just in time," said Kaal, grinning. "Quick, before Jegger gets here."

"What class is this?" John whispered to Emmie, as the three students joined a neat line on the deck. He looked around at the empty space. *Maybe it's PE*, he thought to himself. Running circuits of the vast space would be perfect for long-distance training.

"Shhh," Kaal replied on the other side of him. John looked around to see the huge Derrilian stiffen and stand straighter. "Jegger," Kaal whispered from the corner of his mouth.

A figure was approaching from the far side

of the deck, marching briskly but with a strange, rolling gait. As it came closer, John realized why it looked so odd: Sergeant Jegger had three legs. Two hours earlier John would have gasped in shock, but he had already seen much stranger sights. Besides the extra limb — plus three eyes, one of which was hidden under a patch — the teacher looked almost human, with a bristling moustache and a ring of iron-gray hair around an otherwise bald head.

"Attention!" Sergeant Jegger barked, coming to a halt in front of the line of students. As the students tried to stand even more stiffly, he continued, "Welcome to Intermediate Space Flight, cadets. As you all mastered the basics last term, this term you will be going solo in a class two training dart."

As Jegger spoke, the floor behind him began to revolve and move away. Before John's eyes, a row of spacecraft rose from a holding bay below. Each was made from gleaming metal, shining under the bright lights of the hangar deck. Each ship had a long, sharp nose with a cockpit behind. At the rear were short, sleek, swept-back wings.

Through the clear glass on one ship, John could see what looked like control panels and a large joystick. With a quiet *clonk*, the floor locked into place.

"Let's not waste any time," barked the sergeant. "Board your t-dart. You will find a helmet on each seat. Put it on and fasten your safety harness securely."

"Wonderful!" John heard Emmie Tarz breathe. "Solo flying!" She was already moving toward the nearest craft. Kaal, too, was making for a ship.

"Wait," said John. "Um . . . excuse me,

Sergeant Jegger, sir." His hand shot up. "I've never —"

"Get in your t-dart, cadet," barked the teacher, turning away. "I want everyone in the air in thirty seconds."

"But —"

"Now!"

With a gulp, John walked across the deck toward one of the last two ships. Around him, students were scrambling aboard with whoops of glee. "How hard can it be?" he muttered to himself. "Joystick, control pad. Just like playing a video game." He gulped again as he approached the small craft. "Except that video games don't *actually* fly."

Watching what the other students were doing, John pulled a handle on the side of the ship. The roof of the cockpit slid back. With a hiss, a panel opened in the machine's side, dropping steps. On trembling legs, John climbed in and put on what looked like a metal motorcycle helmet. At once, foam-like material inside it swelled to cushion his head.

As he sat, the flight seat moved forward automatically and the controls dropped until they were within reach. Across the screens in front of him, strange symbols appeared and quickly vanished, replaced with English words. Even so, the electronic panels still looked incredibly complicated. Among the few that John could understand were panels marked "Fuel," "Power," and "Velocity;" other screens showed complicated graphs and what looked like 3-D star maps.

"Preflight checks," said Jegger's voice through his helmet. "Close and lock." John turned his head to see Emmie in the t-dart next to him lean over and pull something near her feet. Looking down, he saw a small lever. He gave it a tug. At once, the steps folded back into their panel and the cockpit door closed overhead.

"Power up your engines!" barked Jegger's voice. "That's to the right of your panel, for anyone who's forgotten over the break."

John stretched out his hand to the touchscreen panel.

"Wait!" snapped Jegger. "Do NOT start engines." Slightly muffled, as if the sergeant were speaking away from the microphone, he continued. "Mordant. Why are you late?"

Through the speakers in his own helmet, John heard Mordant reply from a distance, "I was attending a meeting in Lorem's office." The tone of his voice made it sound as though he and the headmaster had been locked away discussing important business.

Sergeant Jegger wasn't fooled. "In trouble again, cadet?" he snapped.

John couldn't help breaking into a grin inside his helmet as he heard Mordant splutter.

"Save it for someone who cares," Jegger said over Mordant's protests. "Just get in a dart. On the double — you're holding up my class."

A few moments later, Jegger's voice came through clearly again, sounding annoyed. "Right, if everyone is *quite* ready, *power up.*"

John pressed a red glowing panel on the touchscreen and felt his seat begin to vibrate gently. In his helmet, Jegger's voice barked again. "Orders, cadets. Listen up and listen good. As this is your first solo flight, we won't be going any farther than the hangar deck. You'll be flying *very* slowly."

John felt his shoulders sag with relief. He might just be able to handle the t-dart after all.

"Now, let's get moving. Punch the power up to three."

John found the "Power" screen and touched it experimentally. In the top corner the number one flashed and the ship vibrated a little more urgently. John touched the panel twice more until the number changed to three.

"Grip the control stick firmly."

Obeying the instructor, John felt the landing gear fold back into the craft beneath him. It was now hovering a few feet above the deck. Gritting his teeth and feeling a bead of sweat break out on his forehead, John tried to keep the control stick perfectly still.

"Now, one at a time, when I call your name, pull back gently and click back the flight button on top. Ascend to one hundred feet and circle the deck. Ready . . . Tarz, go!"

John watched as Emmie's t-dart tilted and

flew smoothly upward. After leveling off, it began to fly slowly around the hanger.

"Excellent, Tarz," said Jegger, with a tiny hint of approval in his voice. "Rabbus, go. Keep at least fifty feet behind Tarz."

One by one, the t-darts took off. None as smoothly as Emmie Tarz's, but Jegger gave instructions to the pilots until they were flying in good order around the perimeter of the hangar. Soon, only two were left on the deck. "Talliver, go," the sergeant ordered.

As Mordant's craft rose up to join the line of ships, Jegger's voice barked in John's ears again. "*You*. Last cadet. Who are you?"

"John Riley, sir."

"Go, John Riley."

"I-I'm not sure this is a good idea," John stammered.

"I don't want to hear excuses. Get up there."

"But I wasn't here last —"

"Get flying, cadet."

Sudden panic gripped John. The complete craziness of the situation hit him with full force. *What was I thinking? I can't fly a freaking spaceship. The only thing I've ever ridden is a bike.*

He jerked the control stick back. With a lurch, the front of the spaceship swung up until John was blinking at the distant ceiling. "*Gaaah!*" he yelped, his stomach twisting itself in knots.

"Gently! I said *gently!*" an exasperated Jegger bellowed in his ear.

John looked around for a way to escape. Sergeant Jegger glared at him from across the deck, as if he knew exactly what John was thinking and would stuff him back into the cockpit if he tried to get out. There was nothing else for it; he would have to try to fly the ship.

Squeezing his eyes shut, John pushed the

stick away from him a little. The front of the t-dart dipped.

"Better. Now the Flight button."

Half opening one eye and reminding himself to breathe, John flicked the button on top of the control stick. The ship began to move forward.

"Keep the stick firm and fly to one hundred feet. Join the line, keeping plenty of distance between you and the t-dart in front."

The spaceship wobbled alarmingly as John's hands trembled in their grip on the control stick. Gulping a deep lungful of air, he forced himself to relax. The ship stabilized. John moved the control stick slightly to the left until he was moving toward the end of the line.

"I'm flying it," he whispered through clenched teeth. "I'm actually *flying* it." The ship was rolling and tilting, but he was flying. *Awesome.*

"One hundred feet!" barked the voice in his ear, making John jump and the craft roll. Glancing at another panel that gave his altitude, John brought the little spaceship under control and managed to glide in, clumsily, behind Mordant and at the right height.

"All right," said Sergeant Jegger. "That was mostly terrible. Stay in formation for a while, then we'll try some simple maneuvers."

After a few minutes John felt like he was starting to get the hang of flying. The control stick was more sensitive than any video game he had ever played, but the craft was simple to fly and his t-dart flew more smoothly as his confidence increased. When he looked down, he could see the tiny figure of Sergeant Jegger below, giving orders into a microphone. Around the hangar, ships began flipping, turning, and flying a little faster on his command. Kaal's t-dart shot past, and John waved while Kaal gave him a thumbs up.

"John Riley," said Jegger's voice.

With a start, John realized he'd been too busy looking around and hadn't been paying attention to the flight instructor's voice.

"Execute maneuver," came Jegger's voice again.

Panicking, John's eyes swept over the screens. He half-remembered Jegger saying something that sounded like "axle." *What was it?*

Next to the power screen was a large panel with the words "Accelerate boost."

John reached out for the panel as Jegger's voice came again. "What are you waiting for, cadet? Give me an axle roll."

It was too late to correct the mistake. John's fingers were already touching the panel. Beneath him, engines roared suddenly.

The ship leaped forward at a terrifying speed.

"What are you doing?" Jegger's voice roared in his ears, "Slow down, slow down *now*! You're going to hit the —"

John dragged the control stick back only a second before the t-dart crashed into the wall. The spaceship flipped and hurtled back in the opposite direction, with John now flying upside down. Ships scattered as students maneuvered out of its path. He yanked the stick this way and that, trying to avoid them. Within seconds, the ship was rolling uncontrollably as it tore around the hangar.

Sergeant Jegger's voice roared in his ears: "Get a grip, cadet. Pull back, *pull back*. Decrease speed."

Not daring to take his eyes off the view ahead, John reached out and jabbed at the panels blindly, trying to slow down the t-dart while struggling with the control stick to bring it under control.

"Are you trying to kill yourself, you crazy rookie? Cut your speed *NOW*!"

Whatever John pressed made it worse. The ship plunged and spun wildly around the vast hangar. John felt his face freeze in terror. Another wall. He pulled the stick again, forcing the craft to flip once more. Now there was another t-dart directly in his path. John threw the stick forward, but it was too late. For a second he saw Kaal's face, eyes staring and jaw moving as he shouted something. Then a huge crash — the sound of tearing metal.

Everything went black.

* * *

"It's okay, he's just stunned. Move back."

Sergeant Jegger was above him, staring down coldly. "Kaal," John said, gasping. "Is Kaal all right?"

His friend's face moved into view above. "Fine," Kaal said. He grinned, showing off his impressive fangs. "These training ships have amazing safety features."

"What happened up there?" demanded Jegger, pulling John roughly to his feet. "It was a simple maneuver."

"I . . . uh . . . wasn't —" John started. He was about to admit that he hadn't been listening properly when Kaal interrupted.

"It's his first day at Hyperspace High, sir. He's never been on a spaceship before and he didn't do the basic course last semester."

Jegger uttered what John thought must be a curse under his breath. The ship's computer didn't translate it. Glaring down at John, he snapped, "Is *that* what you were trying to tell me?"

John nodded, expecting the sergeant to react furiously. Instead, Jegger looked John up and down, shook his head and said, "My fault, then. Report to me at zero eight hundred hours tomorrow. I'll soon have you up to speed."

"Yes, sir," said John.

"Only not so much speed as today, all right?" Jegger's mouth twitched at the corner.

Before John could reply, the chiming sound he had heard back in Ska's Café rang again.

"Class dismissed!" barked the sergeant.

CHAPTER 7

John was in a gloomy mood and the next class didn't lift it. Kaal and Emmie led him to a laboratory, where Professor Hispus, a four-armed teacher whose head looked like a snake's, was waiting. The class was Advanced Life Form Biology, and John knew he was out of his depth before the professor had even finished the first sentence of his lecture.

Complex charts and symbols flashed across large screens hung around the room as John groaned quietly to himself. While the students around him took out ThinScreens and made notes, John tried to make himself look as small as possible in case the professor asked him a question.

It didn't work.

"You, with the yellow hair next to Kaal, what is your name?" Hispus asked an hour into the lesson.

"John Riley," John replied, sitting up straighter.

"I see you're not taking notes, John Riley, so I can only suppose you must know all this already. Perhaps you could remind the class of the four major differences between the DNA structure of Elvians and Sillarans."

"I'm sorry," replied John. "It's my first day and —"

"The Earthling's as pathetic at biology as he is at flying t-darts," Mordant whispered loudly.

"Maybe they let him into the school to make Tarz look clever for a change."

His hovering Serve-U-Droid spun, lights blinking, at his shoulder, "Yes, Master Talliver. Hyperspace High is supposed to be the most *exclusive* school in the galaxy. One wonders why the headmaster has allowed the primitive to become a student."

John blushed. Emmie and Kaal both glared at Mordant and his rude droid.

"That will do," snapped the professor. "John Riley, see me after class for a reading list. It seems you have a lot to catch up on."

Emmie and Kaal waited outside the door while Hispus gave John a short lecture on being properly prepared, as well as a long list of reading that he should complete before the next class. They looked at him pityingly as he came out a few minutes later, shaking his head.

"I didn't understand a single word," he said glumly. "Talliver's right: I'm pathetic."

"Hey, it's only your first day. You'll catch up," Kaal said cheerfully.

"And it's lunch now," added Emmie. "At least you can take a break."

Lunch, however, was even more depressing. The first-year cafeteria was full of students noisily greeting each other after the holidays. John had to shout to make himself heard over the din. When he took a seat next to Kaal, a compartment slid from the table, serving a plate of foul-smelling purple cubes and a bowl of what looked like frogspawn. Rolling his eyes, John poked at the mess with the metal spike that was by his plate.

"Looks Martian to me!" shouted Kaal, peering over his shoulder. "The computer must still think you're Prince Clo-Ra-Ta. On the plus side, Martian food is supposed to be very good for you."

"If you can keep it down," mumbled John, spearing a purple cube and nibbling it cautiously. It tasted worse than it smelled. Determined to try to cheer up, he put it back in the bowl and yelled, "So what lesson am I going to be awful at next?"

"Plutonian martial arts," replied Kaal, his mouth full of what looked like stew made from peeled worms. He winked. "I'll be gentle with you."

* * *

Two hours later, John staggered out of the padded gym, clutching his ribs. "I'm really, really sorry," said Kaal behind him. "Got a bit carried away there. Don't know my own strength."

"It's all right," panted John. "I don't mind being thrown clear across the room." He paused, then added, "Seven times. I am *so* going to make you pay for that next time."

Kaal's teeth glinted. "It was fun, though, right?" he grinned, slapping John on the shoulder.

"Owww!" John yelped. "Don't touch me. I'm one big bruise."

After a lesson in early galactic history, which again left John with a long reading list and an aching head, the school day was finally over. Wearily, he dragged his stiff, hungry body down to the cafeteria, and then stared with horrified disbelief when the table opened to reveal exactly the same food he'd been given for lunch.

Hoping it wasn't poisonous, he tried the frogspawn this time, but he quickly spit it back into the bowl.

"Yuck," said Emmie Tarz, leaning across the table and wrinkling her nose at his meal. "You should talk to the computer about your food."

"I'll probably be dead from starvation by breakfast," John grumbled in reply.

"I've got roasted falabird with skits and charn salad," she replied. "It's too much for me. Want to try some?"

John leaned over. The food on Emmie's plate smelled better than his own and looked a little like roast turkey with beans the size of his thumb, and orange leaves. "If you're sure you've got enough," he gulped. "I don't want you to go hungry, too."

"Help yourself," she said, smiling.

John spiked some of the falabird and put it in his mouth nervously. The meat was bitter, a long way from delicious, but far better than the Martian gloop in front of him. He swallowed and tried a skit. The large bean tasted like pasta. "Mmmm, thanks," he said, chewing hungrily. "These aren't too bad."

"Do you want to try some of mine?" offered Kaal, who was crunching through a portion of what looked like stir-fried worms.

John quickly shook his head. *Derrilian food looks even worse than Martian food, if that's possible,* he thought.

Pushing his tray away, Kaal sighed.

"I've got that detention now," he said. "Better go, I don't want to upset the Examiners again. Can you find your own way back to the dormitory, John? Or you could hang out in the Center."

"I'd keep you company, but I've got singing practice and a ton of studying," said Emmie apologetically as she stood up. "See you in the morning."

"It's okay. I'd better get started on all this reading. I'll find my own way back."

John groaned as his new friends hurried away.

Ten minutes later he was hopelessly lost. He couldn't even remember his room number, let alone where the dormitory was. Exhausted and despairing, he padded down softly carpeted, empty hallways trying to find his way back to his room. Outside the viewing windows, the glories of the galaxy swept by, but John was in no mood to admire the view. *I'm never going to fit in here*, he told himself.

The hallway suddenly echoed with a chiming sound. A voice said, "John Riley."

John spun around. He was all alone in the dimly lit passage.

"Uh . . . yes?" he said. "Who's there?"

"Ship's computer. The headmaster gave me

instructions to monitor Earth's communications systems. You have received an email. Would you like to read it?"

"I guess so, but I don't have a . . . what do you call them? ThinScreen?"

"That will not be a problem, John Riley."

In the air before John's eyes, an email appeared.

To: john@theRileysHome.com
From: trisha@theRileysHome.com

Re: First Day

Hi John, your dad and I are dying to know about your first day at school. Let us know how it went if you have the time. We miss you already. The house is so quiet without you.

Sending all our love,

Mom

xoxo

PS: Your dad says to tell you that he's going to totally kick your butt at Doom Hammer by the time you get back.

John blinked back sudden tears. His parents were so far away. He hadn't realized how much he was missing them, as well as everything else that he usually took for granted: other human beings, decent food, the sky above his head . . .

The computer interrupted his thoughts. "Would you like to send a reply?"

"Yes, please. How do I do that?"

A new email window opened in the space before him. "Dictate your message," said the computer.

"Hi Mom —" John started, stopping in surprise as his words appeared in the air. After a few seconds, he started again. "It's been a really weird day. It's like I'm a trillion miles from home." As homesickness welled up, he let all his feelings out, telling his parents how out of his depth he felt and that he was the most stupid student in the school. The only thing he left out was that he was, in fact, trillions of miles away from Wortham Court, on a spaceship traveling among distant stars. "Love, John," he finished eventually.

"Sending," the computer told him.

A frown furrowed John's forehead. "Could you tell me how to get back to my dorm?" he asked.

"Of course. You are in dormitory sixteen. There is a TravelTube at the end of this corridor that will take you straight there."

"Thanks." John walked on, silent for a few moments, but hearing a sympathetic voice — even if it belonged to a computer — made him want to talk. "I shouldn't be here," he said gloomily. "Humans are too *primitive*," he added, spitting the word out, "to belong in a place like this."

"Perhaps some music might make you feel better," murmured the computer.

A tune started playing in the background. It was a soothing track sung by a soft-voiced woman. John recognized it instantly. "That's one of my mom's favorites," he said.

"Mine, too. Earth music is excellent," the computer replied. "No species that can make such music could be described as 'primitive.'"

"Well, I *feel* primitive. I'll never catch up with the other students. Anyway, nobody wanted me here. It was just an accident."

"Very little on Hyperspace High happens by accident," the computer responded. "Sometimes it is difficult to understand the headmaster's plans, but he dislikes accidents. As for catching up with the other students, I will help as much as I can."

"That's really kind of you," John said. "Um . . . you're not a *normal* computer, are you? I've never heard of a computer that could have a real conversation."

"I am far more advanced than any computer on Earth," said the computer with — John thought — a trace of pride in its voice. "I am built on a Zero-Electronic Personality Pattern."

"A Zero-Electronic what?"

"Zero-Electronic Personality Pattern. You might call it artificial intelligence," replied the computer. "There are only a few of us in the universe. We were designed by the scholars of

Kerallin to think, to understand, and to *know*, rather than to simply process information like most computers."

In front of John, the door of an elevator — or "TravelTube," as the computer called it — opened. John walked in, so engrossed in the conversation that he barely noticed. The door closed softly as John said, "So you're almost like a *person*?"

"That is an interesting way of putting it," the computer said. "*Almost*, I suppose. The difference is that my mind is hugely superior to your soggy little brain."

John burst into laughter.

"What an interesting sound," said the computer.

"Really?" asked John. "I'm just laughing."

"My databanks tell me that laughter, through increased abdominal activity, releases chemicals into the human brain that enhance positive emotions and suppress pain sensors."

"You mean it makes us feel better," said John.

"That is another way of saying it, yes," said the computer.

"So, what's your name?" asked John through more laughter.

"I am called 'ship' or 'computer,'" replied the voice. "The scholars of Kerallin do not name us."

"But that's ridiculous!" shouted John indignantly. "Everyone should have a name. Would you like me to give you one?"

The voice was silent for a moment. Then, hesitantly, it said, "Yes. Yes, I would like that very much."

"Then from now on you are Zepp. For Zero-Electronic Personality Pattern. How's that?"

The TravelTube doors opened as the computer replied slowly, "Zepp. It is a *good* name."

"Cool," John replied. "So tell me, Zepp, how can you help me catch up with the other students?"

Back in his own dorm room, John kicked off his sneakers and lay back on one of the squishy sofas while he chatted with the computer. For the next hour, the conversation jumped from the school, the headmaster, and the scholars of Kerallin, to Zero-G war and back to Hyperspace High again. The whole time, Zepp gave John information that would come in useful during his time on the vast spaceship. By the time Kaal arrived back from detention, the Earth boy and the computer were in the middle of a heated discussion about pop music.

The green-skinned Derrilian stopped in the

doorway, looking surprised to see John laughing. "Who are you talking to?" he asked, looking around the room.

"Oh, just Zepp," said John with a grin. "Come and join us."

"Well, it's good to see you looking less depressed," replied Kaal, throwing himself onto the sofa opposite and adjusting his wings with a rustle. "But who on Derril is Zepp? Have you gone insane and started talking to yourself?"

"Zepp is the ship's computer. I gave it a name. Kaal, meet Zepp. Zepp, meet Kaal."

"We have spoken before," said the computer, "but we haven't been properly introduced. Good evening, Kaal."

"Oh, hi, computer —"

"Zepp," John corrected.

"Zepp," Kaal said with a frown. "Why are you talking to the computer, John?"

"It's not just a computer. It has a personality. It thinks. It's almost like a person, only —"

"Only with a far superior mind," Zepp interrupted.

"Far superior to our soggy little brains," John agreed with a chuckle.

Kaal blinked. "Oh," he said, looking slightly ashamed. "I didn't know that. And all this time I've been giving it orders like it's just a piece of machinery. I'm sorry about that compu— Zepp."

"It's what I'm here for," Zepp replied. "Though I must say, it is pleasant to have a conversation that isn't just, 'Computer: get me a drink' or 'Computer: set course for Arcachon Five.'"

"We were just talking about music," said John. "Zepp is a big fan of Coldplay, Jay Z, Adele, and the Beatles —"

"What are they?" Kaal asked, looking confused.

"You have much to learn, young Derrilian," said the computer's voice. "But now, it is almost time for lights out. Perhaps you would like some music while you get ready for bed?"

"Hey Jude" by the Beatles began playing.

"So this is Earth music, is it?" asked Kaal, as he stood and held out a hand to help John up from his sofa. "Not bad. And I thought Earthlings were completely useless."

"Next Plutonian martial arts class," John replied with a grin, "I am *so* going to make you pay. You'll see."

The two of them washed and changed, laughing, as John tried to teach Kaal to sing along while Zepp interrupted. Finally, they climbed into their beds as the music faded out and the lights dimmed.

A few minutes later, John sat up and pressed the panel to close the screen to his bed pod. Kaal hadn't been joking: the big Derrilian snored as loud as a cement mixer.

CHAPTER 8

"It is now zero six thirty hours, John Riley. Time to get up."

John lifted his head off the pillow and forced one eye open. The other eye followed quickly. John blinked in surprise as he looked around his bed pod. "Oh, right," he muttered after a few seconds. "Spaceship. Hyperspace High." His head dropped back and he pulled the covers around him. "Just let me sleep another ten minutes, Zepp. Snooze now."

"I have prepared a bath," Zepp's voice

insisted. Cheerful pop music began to play. "You do *not* want to be late for Sergeant Jegger."

John sat bolt upright as he remembered his early flying lesson. "Okay, okay, I'm up. What? Where?"

"I thought you might like to start the day with a bath," repeated the computer.

Zepp had thought right, John decided, as he plunged into the hot water. Immediately, underwater jets began frothing the surface.

"This is amazing," said John, as he kicked off to the other side of the huge tub. "I could stay in here all day."

"But you cannot do that, John. You see, you only have twenty minutes until breakfast," Zepp replied.

"Oh, right, food. I meant to talk to you about the food."

"I have already corrected your menu,"

replied Zepp. "And check the locker by your bed pod when you're finished in here."

Wrapped in a warm towel, and brushing his teeth, John put his hand to the panel that opened the locker. The door slid back. John's toothbrush almost dropped from his mouth.

Yesterday, he'd thrown his backpack into one corner of the empty locker. This morning the locker was full. Shelves to one side held neatly folded underwear, socks, and T-shirts. A collection of clothes and sports gear was arranged on hangers, all in silvery-gray and red colors that John had seen other students wearing. The school colors, he guessed. At the bottom was a rack of brand-new silver sneakers and, next to them, a gleaming ThinScreen, alongside a more familiar-looking bundle of technology. John could hardly believe his eyes.

"Where did you get a copy of Doom

Hammer?" John said, gasping with happiness. "And a console?"

"I made them," said Zepp, sounding a little smug. "Earth electronics are not difficult to copy. I had to make a few adjustments, but the console is now compatible with the ship's screens."

"I-I don't know what to say," John stuttered. "That's really . . . I mean . . . *wow*!"

"Just something to remind you of home, and we cannot allow your father to beat you when you return."

"You are *awesome*. Thanks, Zepp."

* * *

"Double awesome," John said, sighing with pleasure, as the table served his breakfast in the quiet cafeteria. Gone was the Martian gunk.

The tray that rose from the hidden compartment held a large plate loaded with still-sizzling bacon, sausages, scrambled eggs, buttery toast, hash browns, and a dollop of ketchup. Next to the plate were a large glass of fresh orange juice and a steaming mug of hot chocolate.

By the time he had wolfed down the last slice of toast, John felt better than he had since arriving on the ship. Making friends with the computer had turned out to have some serious advantages.

Sergeant Jegger looked at him approvingly as he raced from the TravelTube, right on time for his lesson. "Neat and punctual, Riley!" he barked, moustache bristling. "Both very important in the Starfighter Corps. Let's get on with it, cadet. Board your ship."

John glanced over Jegger's shoulder to where a t-dart was waiting on the deck. The day that had started so well took a sudden dip. He felt his knees sag. "I . . . uh . . . I thought we were going to cover the basics, sir," he babbled. "On the ground, sort of thing."

"Nonsense," snapped the sergeant. "Got to get straight back in the cockpit after a crash or you'll start to *fear* it."

"Like getting right back on a horse," said John, nodding.

The sergeant stared at him blankly. Clearly, they didn't have horses on whichever planet he was from.

"You're wasting time, cadet," said Jegger impatiently.

"Yes sir," said John, slightly less afraid of the t-dart than he was of disobeying the instructor.

Jegger's voice began speaking in his ear even before John had the helmet completely over his head. "Orders, cadet. Listen up and listen good. You'll take off, give me one circuit, then land. Over and over until I'm not thoroughly ashamed to be your instructor. Got that?"

"Yes sir."

"Pre-flight checks!"

The first takeoff was worse than John had managed the day before: the landing almost ended in another crash. But as he practiced, John began to relax. This time, he remembered to concentrate on every word that Jegger said. After half an hour, his takeoffs were almost smooth.

"You've made some progress, cadet," said Jegger, clapping a hand on John's shoulder as he stepped down from the spaceship at the end of the lesson. "Your reactions are good and your control over the dart is improving. Give me another few years and I'll make a starfighter out of you."

John grinned, even though he knew he wouldn't be at Hyperspace High long enough for that to happen.

"Tomorrow we'll start some simple flips and turns, then increase the speed. Give the others a bit of a show by next week, eh?"

As John's jaw fell open, a chime sounded. "Zero eight hundred hours tomorrow, then," said Jegger gruffly. "Off to your next class. Punctuality, that's the thing."

"Zepp, can you hear me?" whispered John, as he watched the sergeant walk away.

"Of course."

"What *is* my next class?"

"The ThinScreen will tell you everything you need to know."

After taking the ThinScreen out of its slim, silver case, John tapped it. At once, it blinked on. An icon in the corner marked "Timetable" flashed once. Another tap and a new screen opened. "0845 hours. Galactic Geography. Doctor Vilkard Graal. Lecture hall F, deck thirty-six," John read. A clock in the corner of the screen told him it was now 0839. Slipping the ThinScreen back in its case, he ran for the TravelTube.

"What's wrong?" John asked Emmie, as he slid into a spare seat between her and Kaal and dropped his ThinScreen on the desk. Emmie's golden skin was pale and she was trembling.

"Not a good class for her," replied Kaal in a whisper, shaking his head.

"My worst," groaned Emmie. "It's Doctor Graal, she's just —"

"Awful," interrupted Kaal. "She's a Gargon. As a species, they can be, well, less than friendly." He nodded toward Mordant, who was leaning back in his chair, looking pleased with himself.

As usual, G-Vez was by his side. "He's half-Gargon. Graal's favorite. You get the idea."

"And I'm useless at Galactic Geography," moaned Emmie, slumping over the desk until her forehead rested on its bright surface. "No matter how hard I study, I can't seem to remember anything."

"Well, look at it this way, Mordant was right about one thing: however bad you are, I'm worse," said John sympathetically. "You won't be bottom of the class at anything while I'm here."

Emmie turned her head toward him, silvery hair falling over one eye. "Like to bet on that?" she asked mournfully.

The door slid open. A great black shape slithered through the door on thick tentacles.

"Good grief, what's that?" yelped John.

"Doctor Graal," whispered Kaal.

"No way," whispered John, shocked. He had seen some strange creatures since coming aboard Hyperspace High, but none were as downright ugly as Doctor Graal.

The great octopus creature reached the desk at the front of the lecture hall and turned to face the students, oozing red eyes sweeping along the rows of desks. Without so much as a "Good morning," Doctor Graal opened her rubbery mouth and, with a stern squelch, said, "We will start the semester with a quiz. Question one: What is the name of the longest mountain range on planet Chole Prime?"

One of Mordant's tentacles shot into the air. John instantly saw the resemblance to Graal.

"Mordant. Yes?"

"The Skivrak Range, Doctor Graal."

"Very good. Where would you find the continent of Mest?"

Mordant's tentacle reached into the air again. "On planet Zelastian."

"Excellent. What is the name of the only known planet to have no land mass above sea level?"

This time, Mordant didn't even put up his tentacle. "P'Sidia!" he shouted.

"Bravo, Mister Talliver," said Doctor Graal, clapping two of her own tentacles together with a slapping noise. "As usual, you are *extremely* well informed. But let us see how well your classmates have prepared. Lishtig ar Steero," she continued, turning to face the purple-haired boy John had met the day before. "The surface of planet Selleticon is formed of what type of rock?"

Lishtig stared at the ceiling, tapping his forehead with one finger. "Wait, I know this," he muttered. "Um, is it sedimentary rock?"

"Correct," said Graal, with obvious distaste. "Emmie Tarz, what process gives gas planets bands of different colors?"

Emmie looked stricken with fear, her face grew even paler, and a bead of pearly sweat broke out on her forehead. "I don't know," she croaked.

The teacher's red eyes glared at her. "Just as I have come to expect. The answer is belt-zone circulation," she rasped. "Perhaps you might know the answer to this one: By what name do we commonly refer to silicate or carbon planets?"

"I'm sorry, Doctor Graal," Emmie replied in a tiny voice, slumping even further in her chair.

John's heart sank as he watched her eyes brim with tears.

"Diamond planets. What is the name of the largest continent on planet Earth?"

Emmie covered her face with her hands as Graal looked around the room. "This is what happens when you don't study," the teacher belched. "But Ms. Tarz will have plenty of time to rectify her lack of attention in detention this evening."

"Oh no," moaned Emmie.

Seeing that Graal was looking away, John leaned toward his friend. For the first time in his life, he felt grateful for geography class back at his old school. "Asia," he whispered in her ear.

Shooting him a look of gratitude, Emmie sat up straighter in her chair and said loudly, "Asia, Doctor Graal."

The doctor turned back to her. "Wrong," she spat. "You really are the most utterly stupid student I have ever taught. The answer is Europolia. Detention starts at —"

"No, it isn't!" shouted John. "The answer is

Asia. There's no such place as Europolia. You mean Europe, which is only the sixth-largest continent on Earth."

A gasp ran around the lecture hall. Several students snickered. From the corner of his eye, John saw Mordant laugh and lean back in his seat with a sneer on his face. Hovering in the air next to his master, G-Vez emitted humorless laughter.

"YOU!" screamed Doctor Graal, glaring at John with pure venom. "What is your name?"

"John Riley," replied John, as calmly as he could manage. "And the correct answer is Asia."

"How dare you question *me*! How dare you tell a teacher she is wrong!"

"I'm sorry, Doctor Graal, but Asia is the largest continent on Earth, and there's no such place as Europolia."

"You'll be expelled for this."

"Why not ask the ship's computer?" suggested John politely. "I have heard that its databanks are infallible."

"Computer," roared the doctor in triumph. "Tell this appalling creature the name of the largest continent on planet Earth. Right now. Immediately!"

Zepp's voice filled the lecture hall. John had to bite his lip to stop himself grinning as the computer announced, "The largest continent on planet Earth is Asia."

A stream of gray drool ran from Graal's mouth. Hatred burned in her red eyes. Her massive body trembled with rage.

"The sixth-largest continent on planet Earth is named Europe," continued Zepp. "There is no continent called Europolia."

Seconds ticked by in stunned silence. No one in the room dared to breathe. Doctor Graal stared at John until he felt that her eyes would burn through the back of his head. Nevertheless, he refused to drop his own gaze.

Abruptly, her great octopus-like bulk shifted. Turning away, the doctor roared, "ThinScreens out! Read the first three chapters of Helius Ka-trill's *Continental Development in Various Planet Types*. I want an essay from every student by the beginning of the next lesson."

As Emmie bent to pick up her ThinScreen, she gave John the most dazzling smile he had ever seen, whispering, "Thank you."

John could feel his cheeks flushing. Just then, Kaal's huge elbow smashed into his ribs in what the Derrilian probably thought was a gentle nudge. Kaal winked as John turned his head.

Even so, John felt his gloominess return. Something told him he had just made a big mistake — and an enemy.

CHAPTER 9

With his chin in his hands, John stared at words scrolling across a large screen in the ship's library. "Zepp," he groaned, "can't you just download all this stuff straight into my brain? I won't mind. Honestly."

"I could do that," said Zepp, causing John to sit up in his chair, hope flashing in his eyes. "If you had an elegantly designed electronic brain," the computer continued, "and not a messy chunk of jelly."

John rolled his eyes and slumped back,

muttering, "Great. Thanks. Now I feel so much better."

Sighing, he stared around the library. It was a beautiful room, lined with paintings and ancient books in glass cabinets, probably far too precious ever to be taken out and read. Soft lighting showed empty desks. As usual, John was the only person in the room. Students could access all the information they needed from anywhere on the ship and most preferred to work in their own dormitories. John had only started working in the library at Zepp's suggestion. It was quiet and peaceful, with no distractions like Kaal asking him for a game of Zero-G war.

By now, John was starting to hate the place. When he wasn't in class or eating, he had been spending every waking hour in the library for the past seven days. Even while the rest of the school was enjoying the weekend, he had been hunched in front of a screen from breakfast until lights-out.

"You've learned a lot in a week," Zepp said more seriously. "In some subjects, you've caught up with the rest of the class."

John nodded. Math had been easy. Numbers were the same throughout the universe and he had always been good at math. His talent had been the reason Wortham Court School had offered him a scholarship. Zepp had introduced him to some new mathematical ideas, but they hadn't taken long to understand.

But the other subjects were a problem. Before he could even start the mountain of homework various teachers had handed out, he had had to start from scratch in almost every subject, beginning with work the other students had covered years before. Even with Zepp patiently explaining, it had been a struggle. John was sure all the information he was trying to fit inside his head would soon make it explode.

"Let's just go over these chapters on the early development of hyperspace technology again, then we'll make a start on the history of the First Galactic Council," said Zepp.

As pages he had already read three times reappeared on screen, John muttered under his breath and leaned in closer, hand poised over his ThinScreen to take notes.

An hour later, the screen suddenly went blank. "Lunchtime," Zepp announced. "Let's pick up from here after you've had something to eat."

"Are you sure you don't mind helping me? I'm sure you've got more important things to do."

Zepp said, "My processors are more than capable of multitasking. Who did you think was flying the ship while I was tutoring you? I am very happy to assist you in any way I can."

"Actually, there is something else," said John.

By now, John was finding his way around the vast ship more easily. Instead of taking a TravelTube to the cafeteria, he returned to his own room. It was empty.

"Good, Kaal's at lunch," he said, taking his old clothes out of the locker and getting changed. Sitting cross-legged on his bed, he checked over his shoulder. Only a blank wall. There was nothing that could give away the fact that he was on a spaceship and not at a boarding school. "Ready, Zepp?" he whispered.

"Patching in to the Internet. It's *ridiculously* slow," Zepp replied. "Ah, here we are — Skype."

The entertainment screen by John's bed switched on, showing the Skype homepage. Zepp had already put in a call.

Far across the universe, a mouse clicked "Answer."

"John! Is that you?"

His mom's face appeared on the screen. John blinked and tried to smile. "Hi, Mom. It's great to see you."

"It's good to see you, too," she replied.

His dad appeared next to her. They were both in their pajamas, but John had no way of knowing whether it was morning or night on Earth. "Hello, son. How's Wortham Court?"

"Okay," said John. Wishing he could tell his parents the truth about his new school, he added, "But I'm way behind. Spending most of my time catching up in the library."

His parents glanced at each other, frowning. "That doesn't make sense, John. You did well at your last school. You shouldn't be that far behind," said his dad.

John shrugged. "There are a lot of new subjects."

"Are you settling in yet?" his mother asked.

"Have you made any friends?" his father cut in.

John had been planning to tell his parents that everything was fine, but seeing them reminded him again of how much he missed home. His smile faded. "Friends?" he said, realizing that he'd hardly spoken to Kaal, or anyone else apart from Zepp, for the last week. "Yes, I think so. But everyone here is . . . um . . . different. I'm not sure I fit in."

"Different how?" asked his dad.

For a second John wondered what would happen if he told his parents he was sharing a room with a seven-foot-tall alien who looked exactly like a demon.

Wishing he hadn't said anything, he mumbled,

"Oh, you know, just new people I haven't met before."

"You look unhappy, John," said his mom with another frown. "You can always come home if you don't like the school."

John shook his head. It would be impossible to cross the light-years that separated him from his parents. "It's okay," he answered. "I've just been working hard. I'm sure I'll start enjoying it more once I'm used to it. Anyway, I just wanted to say hi. I'd better get back to the library."

"You're studying on a Sunday morning?" His mom sounded horrified. "Can't you at least take a couple of hours off?"

"I just want to catch up with this stuff about the First Galacti— I mean, Ancient Rome."

"Good grief, that sounds boring."

John found himself smiling. "Believe me, it *is*," he said.

After a short goodbye, John changed back into his school clothes. His mother had ended the call quickly, but not quickly enough to keep him from seeing a tear rolling down her face. He hated to worry his parents and silently promised himself that he would be more cheerful next time he spoke to them, no matter what it took. After all, being at Hyperspace High was an opportunity that no other human had ever experienced.

"You should get back to the library," Zepp's voice said eventually.

"I know, I know. We've still got to get through the First Galactic Council," John replied, sighing.

Even though much about Hyperspace High was different from schools on Earth, one thing was the same — doing homework on the weekend was a drag. And if he was only going to be at Hyperspace High for a few more weeks, it felt like a shame to spend his time working in the library instead of having fun with his classmates. It wasn't as if his grades in Galactic Geography or Cosmic Languages would mean anything back on Earth.

But it wasn't in John's nature not to try his best, so he picked up his ThinScreen and headed to the library.

CHAPTER 10

"There you are," said Kaal, flapping his wings as the library door slid open. "Zepp said you'd be here. We've been waiting for*ever*."

"Five minutes, at least," Emmie Tarz added. She was sitting on a desk, swinging her legs and looking around the library with interest. "You know," she said, "I didn't realize Hyperspace High even *had* a library."

"That's no big surprise," said Kaal.

Emmie turned to him with a glint in her eye. "Hey, what's *that* supposed to mean?"

"Well, you're not a library kind of girl are you, Tarz?" said Kaal, grinning.

"And when was the last time you were up here, Mister Brainbox?" Emmie shot back.

"Hi," interrupted John, looking from the big Derrilian to Emmie. "Did you want something, or did you just come up here to argue?"

"We wanted something," answered Kaal. "You tell him, Emmie."

Pushing a strand of hair behind her slightly pointed ears and giving John another dazzling smile, Emmie said, "I didn't get to say thanks properly for helping me in Galactic Geography."

"There's no need to —"

"Shut up, I haven't finished yet," said Emmie, switching her smile to a stern look in an instant. "Also, you've been on your own up here all week, studying." She made a face. "Yuck. So we've organized a treat for you."

"That's really kind of you, but I've got to finish —"

"No, you don't," Zepp cut in. "There's no history lesson tomorrow. It can wait."

"You see," said Kaal, "No excuses. You've been stuck up here being boring all week. We started to forget what you look like. So now it's time for some fun. Emmie's spoken to Sergeant Jegger and —"

"And he's letting me take out a Star Racer for two hours," finished Emmie proudly. "First years aren't supposed to, but he said I'm an *exceptional* pilot."

"What's a Star Racer?" asked John, as he looked from Emmie's bright, excited eyes to Kaal's grin.

* * *

"*This* is a Star Racer," announced Emmie as they stepped out of a TravelTube and onto the hangar deck.

John felt his jaw fall open. In the middle of the deck, a spaceship was waiting. A spaceship that looked as though it had been built for speed. Long and sleek and shining beneath the lights of the hangar, it was much larger than the t-darts that John was now getting used to. Behind the cockpit, the ship looked like it was one big engine.

Noticing John's stare, Emmie said, "It's a small version of Hyperspace High's engine. Very, *very* fast," she added.

"Come on, then," said Kaal impatiently, ducking under one of the ship's stubby wings. "I'll drive."

"You will NOT!" Emmie yelled, running for the boarding steps.

The engine was already thrumming by the time John sank into the seat next to Emmie's and pulled a harness over his shoulders. The cockpit lid closed and locked above his head. "Okay," he heard her whisper, "Let's see what you've got." Flicking a switch on the control panel in front of her, she said loudly, "Pre-flight checks complete, sergeant. Ready to fly."

Jegger's voice rang through the cockpit. "You're clear, Tarz. Two hours. Not a second longer."

"Yes sir."

Ahead, huge bay doors slid back. Emmie nudged the stick between her knees and the Star Racer's engines throbbed. With the flick of another switch, the ship began moving forward.

"Ready?" Emmie asked.

"Ready," answered John.

"Get a move on, Tarz," Kaal said.

"You asked for it." Emmie pushed the control stick forward again. Behind John, the engine noise increased to a roar. The ship leaped forward, sweeping out into space. "Yeehah!" Emmie said, twisting the stick. The Star Racer rolled, spinning its passengers like a washing machine.

"That will do, Tarz," said Jegger. "*Sensible* flying. I want her back in one piece."

"No problem, sir. See you in two hours," replied Emmie, pushing the stick again. With jets burning, the ship plunged forward. Turning her head, Emmie asked, "Ever been through a nebula?" She smiled as John shook his head. "You're going to like this, then. Engaging hyperdrive in three, two, one . . ."

Stars streamed by as the Star Racer flashed through space, engines now pulsing quietly. Ahead, John saw a vast cloud of pink and yellow.

It was shaped like a dragon in flight and glowed with a billion lights.

"Isn't it beautiful?" whispered Kaal. "Nebulae are where stars are born. Planets, too."

"It's amazing," John said, as they plunged into the glowing cloud. Space lit up like shining cotton candy. *I am*, he reminded himself, *the first human being ever to see this.*

It was an awe-inspiring moment; a moment that would have been even more awe-inspiring if Kaal hadn't been next to him yelling, "Come on, Emmie! Faster! You pilot like a little old Wussian."

Zepp's voice cut in. "Ms. Tarz, if you take your ship eighteen degrees mark eight point two-two-five, you will find a new solar system forming. Be careful, there is a lot of asteroid activity in the area."

Like Kaal, Emmie had started speaking more politely to the ship's computer since John had told her its name. "Will do. Thanks, Zepp," she said, changing course.

A few moments later, Emmie swerved the ship around a lump of rock and ice the size of a skyscraper that was spinning through space. In the distance, a star burned bigger and brighter than the thousands of others John could see. It didn't hold his attention for long. "What's that?" he asked excitedly, pointing out of the viewing window at a great ball of swirling gas.

"You've seen me in Galactic Geography, right?" said Emmie with a shrug. "Ask Kaal."

"I think it's a baby gas planet," said Kaal slowly. "By the time it's fully formed, it will be four or five hundred times the size of your Earth. Look, it's got bands of different colors already. Belt-zone circulation, Tarz," he finished.

"Ugh, don't remind me of Graal," groaned Emmie. "Let's go farther in." She pulled the ship around another huge asteroid.

"Another planet," said Kaal, pointing. Through the window, the star was now so big that John thought it must be a sun. His gaze followed Kaal's pointing finger. Hanging in space to one side of the ship, lit up by the sun's light, was a vast ball of molten rock, glowing red.

"Wow," he whispered. Emmie swerved the ship to skim past for a better view. As John watched, a massive asteroid hurtled into the new planet, throwing up a huge spout of lava that collapsed slowly back. "That is totally the coolest thing I have ever seen. *Ever*," he said.

"Incredible, isn't it?" whispered Kaal. "One day, that planet will probably have land and oceans. It might evolve life."

"Well, this has been fun, but I feel the need for speed," Emmie said with a giggle, flipping the Star Racer and dodging past more asteroids toward clear space. "John, Jegger said that your piloting has really improved. Do you want to take the controls?"

"Let me think about that . . . uh . . . *YES*. I definitely do. But what about you? Don't you want to pilot?"

"I'll do it next time," shrugged Emmie. "This is *your* treat."

They swapped seats. "The controls are similar to the t-dart's," Emmie explained, leaning over him. And the sensors say there's only clear space ahead, so you don't have to worry about hitting anything."

Glancing around at Emmie and Kaal, John chuckled and asked, "Did someone ask for speed?" Without waiting for an answer, he reached out, punched the panel up to one hundred, and threw the control stick forward. The engine roared.

"*Whoooooooa!*" John yelled as the craft blasted forward. "This is *awesome!*"

"I told you I'd give you a treat," Emmie shouted back. "Think it can go any faster?"

"Only one way to find out," said John, reaching for the "Accelerate Boost" panel.

Burning through space in this racer among stars that no other human would ever see, John's earlier worries slipped away. Whatever else happened on Hyperspace High, he decided, it was all worth it for this single moment. It didn't matter if he got the worst grades in every class, or if every teacher hated him; he would happily go through all that and worse to feel the controls of a faster-than-light spaceship in his hands as he soared through space.

For a moment, John thought about joining the Starfighter Corps, like Sergeant Jegger. Then he would be able to do this every day. With a jolt, he remembered that within a few weeks he would be leaving Hyperspace High and returning to Earth. The closest he would come to this feeling again would be flying spaceships in computer games.

"Two hours is up in ten minutes," said Emmie at last, interrupting his thoughts. "Better head back."

"Thanks, Emmie. Thanks, Kaal," John panted as he brought the speed down and unfastened his harness. "That was the most fun I've ever had. The best present anyone has ever given me."

"Oh, shut up," said Kaal, looking away shyly. "It was nothing."

"Jegger's right," said Emmie. "You're a

natural pilot. With a little more practice, you could be pretty good."

As Emmie took her seat and steered the racer back to Hyperspace High, John looked from her to Kaal. *Yeah*, he thought, *I've made some friends. Some really excellent friends.*

CHAPTER 11

John raced along the hallway. The first lesson of the day was Galactic Geography and he wanted to go over his notes one more time before Doctor Graal arrived. As he ran, he repeated to himself some of the facts he had learned with Zepp over the last week. "The longest river in the galaxy is Great Fluvia on planet Arnis. The tallest mountain is Mount Gijian on Hult-Gorath, named after the planet's twelfth king —"

"Galactic Geography. Fascinating subject," said a voice alongside him.

John skidded to a halt as a flashing ball of light burst into the shape of the headmaster. "Good morning, sir," he panted.

"And a good morning to you, John Riley," replied the headmaster brightly. "Here's a nugget of information for you: Last month the Churl discovered a small, uninhabited planet in the Delta Region. Very dull, of no real interest to anyone. They named its five continents: Klist, Andarus, Jax North, Jax South, and Korus."

"Klist, Andarus, Jax North, Jax South, and Korus," John repeated, confused. "Okay. Thank you, sir."

"*Excellent*. But I don't wish to make you late, so let us walk together," Lorem continued, striding off down the hallway, smiling and nodding to passing students.

"I want to congratulate you on making such a great effort in the time you've been with us," the headmaster said as John caught up. "The computer, or Zepp, as it now likes to be called" — he flashed John a smile — "tells me that you have worked hard. Several teachers say you made good progress considering the subjects were completely new to you. You have a natural gift for mathematics and Sergeant Jegger thinks you could be a superb pilot."

Blushing, John said, "Well, the classes are a lot more interesting than back on Earth. Some of them, anyway," he added truthfully. Then he thought about what the headmaster had said. "Hey, hang on," he blurted. "You said 'in the time you've been with us' but it's weeks before we get to Earth. You're not going to throw me out an airlock again, are you?"

"Goodness, no," Lorem replied with a chuckle. Changing the subject abruptly, he continued. "Let me tell you about seeing the future, John Riley. Sometimes it is crystal clear. At other times, clouded. There are often a number of different possibilities, any one of which might or might not happen."

"I see," said John, wondering why Lorem was telling him this.

"You are wondering why I am telling you this."

John's eyes widened in surprise.

The headmaster chuckled. "A lucky guess. I'm not a mind reader."

"Well, yes, I was thinking that," John admitted.

"Something that I hoped would not happen *has* happened," the headmaster said. He sighed. "A star recently went supernova in the sector of the galaxy into which we were heading." He waved his hand, as if answering a question that John hadn't asked. "That's not a big problem.

It happens all the time. But it was in a heavy star cluster and set off a chain reaction. So far, more than a thousand stars have exploded and more will follow. There is now a possibility that a supermassive black hole will form."

John had no idea what a supermassive black hole was, but it sounded bad. "Is anyone in any danger?" he asked.

"There are no populated planets in the region, and there's no real danger to the ship, either. But to be on the safe side, I've ordered a change of course."

"How does that affect me?"

"It means that we will be passing close to Earth much sooner than expected," Lorem explained. "So we will be able to take you home the day after tomorrow."

"Oh," said John, taken aback. "That's . . . uh . . . that's great. Thank you for telling me,

Headmaster." He blinked. The news should have made him happy, but for some reason it didn't. He would miss Kaal and Emmie, he realized, and flying t-darts. It was unlikely that he would ever fly a spaceship again.

"What is it, John?" asked Lorem quietly, stopping and turning to look at him closely.

"Everything will be back to normal again," John said, frowning. "But I was just getting used to everything *not* being normal. That is, it's been difficult getting used to Hyperspace High, and I've missed home, but in the last week I've seen things and done things that no one from my planet could even imagine." John looked down at his feet. "It will be hard to give that up. After Hyperspace High, school on Earth is going to seem a bit boring."

"In that case, John Riley," Lorem said softly, "You will be pleased to know that Hyperspace

High still has an adventure in store for you before we reach Earth." He held up a hand as John began to question him. "It is *very* clouded," he said firmly. "I honestly cannot tell exactly what will happen. And even if I knew, telling you might change the course of events in a way that would not end well for you."

"So is this goodbye, Headmaster?" said John sadly.

"It is goodbye . . . for now," Lorem answered, as he twinkled into a ball of light. "Now, you have a class, I believe."

Leaving John standing in the hallway, the ball of light shot away and disappeared through a wall.

* * *

"Rantoo-styl-Agabo," snapped Doctor

Graal in her blubbery voice. "What name do we give to a forested world?"

John doodled on his ThinScreen. Graal, it seemed, liked quizzes. It gave her a chance to heap praise on her favorites and ridicule the students she didn't like. So far she had avoided him, Emmie, and Kaal, so he didn't much care. He would be going home in two days anyway. Whatever Doctor Graal thought of him, it didn't matter now.

"An *arboreal* planet," replied Rantoo quickly, her eyes weaving at the end of long stalks.

"Correct. Well done. Flar Hannick, which planet is home to the Shem Ice Caves?"

"Stalica Six, Doctor Graal."

"Incorrect," the teacher belched. "It is Stalica Five. Study harder. One point deducted from your essay grade!"

As the doctor's questions continued, John's

mind drifted. He was going home. That meant he would be going to Wortham Court first or his parents would find out that he had never been there. His stomach sank as he realized he would have to settle in to a new school all over again. Glancing at Kaal and Emmie on either side of him, he wondered if he would make such good friends again. *Probably not.*

"Correct again! Excellent, Mordant. I wish other students would follow your example. Now, John Riley, what is the name of Hella Minor's moon?"

With a start, John's attention snapped back to the octopus-like teacher. "Uh —" he said.

"Just as I thought," sneered Graal. "If the question isn't about your own backward little planet, you haven't got a clue."

John scowled. For a moment he thought about telling Doctor Graal where she could stick her stupid quiz. In two days he would never see her again. But that, he decided, would just make her even more unbearable. Plus, he didn't want to spend his last two days in detention. "Glaymus," he remembered just in time. "Hella Minor's moon is called Glaymus."

The doctor spluttered, reeling back on her tentacles. "Y-yes. Glaymus. Correct. Perhaps you could tell the class what caused the triple planet of Alias-Kush-Mirian to form."

John racked his brain. He had read about Alias-Kush-Mirian a few days earlier, but he had read so much it was difficult to remember every detail.

"The answer, John Riley?" Graal pressed.

"An enormous meteor strike split the planet into three smaller ones," John blurted.

"Correct. Why is Kush such an important planet?" Graal asked.

Kaal's hand shot up, his wings rustled angrily. "Can you ask the rest of us some questions, Doctor Graal?"

"Silence!" Graal roared in reply. "I am the teacher here. I will question whomever I like. I am waiting, Mister Riley."

John stared at her in silence for a moment, thinking back to his study sessions with Zepp. Then he quietly said, "It has large deposits of the rare metal mallux, used in making spaceships."

Graal slobbered venomously. Drool ran from her mouth. "Correct," she muttered bitterly.

Another question followed. Then another. John sat straighter, arms on the desk before him as he answered each with growing confidence. The hours spent staring at a screen in the library were paying off.

"You seem to have picked up a few simple facts," said Graal eventually. "No more than I would expect from a small child on any *civilized* planet, but quite impressive for your species, I suppose."

John smiled thinly at her. "Thank you, Doctor Graal," he said coldly. He refused to get angry.

"One final question," continued the teacher. "A question more suited to a class at this level." Drawing a noisy breath, she sneered, "If I remember correctly, you enjoy naming continents. Please tell us the names of the five continents on the new planet recently discovered by the Churl in the Delta Region."

"That's not *fair!*" shouted Emmie suddenly, already halfway out of her seat. "No one knows that. It was only discovered last month. It's not in any of the textbooks. I only heard about it because my father —"

"You will *sit down*, Tarz," Graal howled.

Turning back to John, she said, "Well, Mister Riley?" with triumph in her voice.

John remembered what Lorem had told him. Silently, he thanked the headmaster. For a moment, he stared at the teacher. Then he smiled. "The continents are called Klist, Andarus, Jax North, Jax South, and Korus, Doctor Graal," he said politely.

"*Yessss*," he heard Kaal and Emmie hiss together under their breath. John didn't dare look at them in case he started laughing.

"That is the end of the quiz," said Graal, without even bothering to tell the class that John had answered correctly.

"That was *amazing*," Kaal whispered across the desk. "How did you know *that*?"

"Tell you later," John whispered back.

"Silence!" Graal shouted again, glaring at them. "Now, I have some important news," she continued. "You may have heard that the ship has changed course. We are now headed in a direction that will take us close to the planet Zirion Beta. Mordant, perhaps you could tell us what is interesting about Zirion Beta."

"Zirion Beta is completely covered with volcanoes, Doctor Graal," answered Mordant with a smirk.

"Very good, Mordant. An extra point for your essay."

Staring around at the rest of the class, she continued, "As Mordant says, Zirion Beta is a highly volcanic planet. Once every seven hundred and seventy-three years, all of its volcanoes erupt at exactly the same time — an event known as the Mega-Eruption. Luckily for us, the Mega-Eruption is due tomorrow, so I have arranged a field trip. You will all be joining me to watch one of the most spectacular sights in the universe from a shuttle orbiting Zirion Beta."

As an excited murmur spread around the class, John groaned quietly. Tomorrow he would see one of the most spectacular sights in the universe. But after that, it would all be over. He would be back home. Emmie, Kaal, and Hyperspace High would be a distant memory — one he couldn't tell anyone about. Ever.

CHAPTER 12

The next day, the shuttle hangar was already abuzz as John stepped out of the TravelTube with Emmie and Kaal. Students clustered around the shuttle, shouting, sharing jokes, and rummaging through the packed lunches that had been delivered with their breakfast trays.

"Ugh," moaned Gobi-san-Art in his low, gravelly voice. "I've got granite bars. I *hate* granite bars. Anyone want to swap?"

"Hey, Riley," said Lishtig, slapping John on the back. "That's twice you've made Doctor

Slobber look like an idiot. Nice work. What's next? Going to push her into a volcano?"

"Good idea, but I was planning to spend the trip hiding under a seat," replied John with a grin.

"*Excellent*, you'll be doing us all a favor," drawled a voice behind him.

"Oh, *very* witty, young Master Talliver," droned another voice.

"Shut your big mouth, Mordant. And tell your pathetic droid to shut up, too," snapped Emmie, whirling around.

"Gosh, that really put me in my place. You're *so* smart, Tarz," sneered the black-haired boy. "I heard the headmaster was lying about the supermassive black hole. The real reason he changed course was so that we could get your pet Earthling off the ship as soon as possible."

"At least I won't have to look at your face

anymore," John snapped back. "But I'll probably have nightmares about it for years."

"Maybe you should take your pals with you," replied Mordant. "They'd fit in well among the lower life forms."

"Oh *bravo,* Master. Your wit is as sharp as a Gargon battleblade today," intoned G-Vez.

"Why don't you just take Emmie's advice and shut it for once, Talliver," interrupted Kaal in a low growl. "Everyone was having a good time until you and your freaky droid showed up. It's an adventure, you know."

An adventure? John thought to himself. Was this what Lorem had meant when he said that Hyperspace High still had an adventure in store for him?

As Mordant opened his mouth to reply, a wet-sounding voice bellowed, "*Siii*-lence!" from the TravelTube. The doctor had arrived.

Slapping two tentacles together, she quickly ordered the class to form a neat line.

"Out of my way," said Mordant, pushing students aside to get to the front of the line.

"Watch where you're going," snapped Queelin Temerate, as she was shoved backward by a tentacle in the chest.

"I said *silence*, Temerate," blubbered the teacher, as she slithered toward the shuttle's door, "Ahh, Mordant, you're first in line. It makes me very happy to see such an excited student."

Once her students finished jostling for the best seats, the doctor engaged the shuttle's autopilot and ordered her pupils to take out their ThinScreens. "In your message boxes," she said, "you will find an excellent article on Zirion Beta I wrote for *Intergalactic Geographic Journal*. We have a long flight ahead of us, so even the slower students will have time to read it." She gave Emmie Tarz a meaningful glance.

Quiet groans filled the shuttle as screens were switched on. John rolled his eyes as he read the first line of what looked like a very long essay: *As many readers will know, I was recently awarded the prestigious Sarbola Prize for my groundbreaking work on volcanic planets. . . .*

"Loves tooting her own horn, doesn't she?" whispered Kaal in the next seat.

"Still doesn't know what the biggest continent on Earth is, though," said Emmie, staring angrily at the back of Graal's huge head. "Maybe John should get the Sarbola Prize."

Engine humming, the shuttle lifted off the deck and out through the hangar bay doors. Picking up speed, it swooped once around Hyperspace High and out into space. John tore his eyes away from the star-strewn view outside the window and tried to concentrate on Graal's article. The "adventure" wasn't starting too well, but he had to admit that the idea of seeing a whole planet of volcanoes erupting was pretty exciting. It would be another sight no other human would ever witness.

Maybe Lorem was right, John thought to himself, pulling his knees up and resting the screen against them. *This could still be an amazing adventure.*

The shuttle cruised through space, silent apart from the rustling of packed lunch bags, muffled snorts of laughter, and whispered conversations that Graal quickly silenced with a red-eyed glare. For four hours, John struggled through the article. A small part of him wondered why he was bothering when he would soon be back on Earth, trillions of miles away from Doctor Graal.

She'll probably give a quiz later, he reminded himself.

"Approaching planet Zirion Beta. Orbit in two minutes," the shuttle's computer broke in eventually.

"At last," breathed Kaal, switching off his ThinScreen and tucking it into a bag at his feet. "I was about to actually die of boredom."

"I understood the first sentence. After that it might as well have been written in ancient Helvian," complained Emmie.

Doctor Graal squirmed her way to the front of the shuttle and pointed a tentacle to a small brown and orange ball ahead. "Zirion Beta," she said with a burp. "By my calculations, there should be just over two hours before the Mega-Eruption begins. Once we have entered orbit, we will pass the time with a quiz on my article before lunch."

Again, several students groaned.

"Establishing low orbit one hundred miles above the surface of planet Zirion Beta," announced the shuttle's computer.

John looked out the viewing window, realizing he'd been lucky to get a seat on the left side of the craft. The planet's surface filled the window like a huge model of the alien world. He would be one of the few to have a completely clear view. The windows across the aisle showed only space.

A second later, John wasn't so sure of his luck. Students from the other side of the aisle crammed over for a better view. "Hey! Back off, Werril," he grunted, as one of the Klopian's horns jabbed him in the side of the head.

"Sorry, John," murmured Werril, pulling his head away a little.

John returned his gaze to the viewing window.

Below, the planet spun slowly. It was a brown, craggy, threatening place, with no suggestion that life might exist on its surface. Great cracks ran across a rough landscape; vast volcanoes belched smoke that quickly whipped away on high winds. Molten lava was already running down the slopes of many peaks, forming lakes of fire.

"Return to your seats!" shouted Graal. "There will be plenty of time —"

She never finished the sentence. An enormous crash sent the shuttle spinning. Screams and shouts filled the air. Squealing, Doctor Graal tumbled around the craft, along with the students who had released their safety harnesses.

"*Whaaaa!*" shrieked the teacher, as another *thud* set the shuttle whirling in the opposite direction.

"Warning: Asteroid strike. Warning: Asteroid strike," the computer droned loudly, its alarm blaring.

Eyes wide, John glanced out the window. Outside, space whirled crazily. One second the planet's surface filled the screen, the next, stars. From the corner of his eye, John caught sight of a basketball-sized rock spinning toward the craft. Fresh screams filled the shuttle as the asteroid hit with a dull thud, followed by the shriek of breaking metal.

"Autopilot error. Orbit failing. Emergency stabilizers online," warned the computer. "Abandon shuttle. Abandon shuttle."

As the jets suddenly stopped roaring, the craft stopped spinning. A hatch hissed opened at the rear. Shooting a quick look out the window while he unfastened his harness, John saw more rocks tumbling toward them. His face paled. Another rock might hit the craft at any moment, and if one of the viewing windows was smashed, everyone inside would be sucked out into space instantly.

"Let me through! Let me *through!*"

John's head whirled at the sound of the croaking shriek. Doctor Graal was fighting her way along the central aisle, tentacles curling around crying students and thrusting them out of her path. "The escape pod!" she screamed. "We must get to the escape pod! Everyone form a line behind Mordant."

Shoving two students out of her path, the teacher squeezed her bulk through the hatch. "I'm trained for these situations," she babbled. "I'll just enter the launch code. Everyone line up behind Mordant."

John frowned. Surely Doctor Graal shouldn't be boarding the escape pod ahead of her students. The panicking teacher was hardly setting a good example.

Mordant forced himself down the aisle through a mad scuffle. "You heard her!" he screeched. "I'm first. Everyone behind me."

John could see the Gargon inside the pod, jabbing wildly with her tentacle at a control panel.

Instantly, the hatch hissed closed. With a metallic crunch, the pod detached from the shuttle and blasted away to safety.

"Escape pod away," droned the computer. "Autopilot error. Orbit failing. Collision with planet Zirion Beta in two minutes."

"She left us!" screamed Queelin Temerate. "Doctor Graal's left us to *die*."

"It must have been an accident!" wailed Mordant above the screams. "She would never leave us."

"Shut up, Talliver! Graal's gone and we're going to crash," said Lishtig.

There was a flurry of activity in the seat next to John. "Not if I've got anything to do with it!" shouted Emmie grimly. "I just need to get to the manual override."

As she stood up, Mordant lunged forward and pushed her back into her seat.

"*No*. Doctor Graal *is* coming back for us!" he screamed into her face. "She'll be back any second."

"Graal's not coming back, you idiot," grunted Kaal, exploding out of his own seat and flinging Mordant across the aisle.

As Mordant crashed against the window, his droid immediately buzzed over and started straightening his clothes. "If you wish to fight the Derrilian again, sir," it said, sounding as unflappable as ever, "may I suggest a quick punch to the jaw followed by a flurry of sharp jabs."

Mordant's only answer was a sob of anguish.

By now John, too, was on his feet. "Listen!" he bellowed into the screams. "Emmie's the best pilot here. If anyone can get us down, it's her. But we have to be calm and let her through."

His words had the desired effect. Every student clutched at the tiny branch of hope that John was holding out. The screaming died down.

With a grateful glance over her shoulder, Emmie dived for the front of the shuttle, students hurrying out of her path.

"Collision with planet Zirion Beta in ninety seconds," the ship's computer announced.

With John close behind, Emmie stabbed at a red button by the shuttle door. A panel slid back at chest height, revealing a small control stick and flight panel. She instantly punched at a panel marked "Distress Beacon."

"Need any help?" John asked, panting. Ahead, the planet loomed even larger than before. He tried not to look at the rocky volcanic surface spinning beneath, its gravity pulling the struggling shuttle ever closer.

"No. Just keep them quiet," Emmie said without looking at him. Her eyes fixed on the large viewing window ahead, Emmie curled her fingers around the control stick while her other hand pressed "Emergency Manual Override."

The craft shuddered and seemed to threaten to begin spinning again. Yanking at the control stick and cursing under her breath, Emmie fought to stabilize it. "Entering the atmosphere," she muttered.

As the shuttle bucked and shuddered, the screaming began again. John whirled around.

Halfway down the aisle, Kaal was looking after Rantoo, who was moaning and clutching her head. Even from a distance, John could see yellow blood trickling down her face.

"It's *okay*!" yelled John. "We've just hit the planet's atmosphere, it's going to get bumpy. Stay calm and we'll all get through this."

Behind him Emmie cursed again. This time John heard fear in her voice. "Engine's hit," she gasped. "There are only stabilizers. I can't slow her down."

The floor beneath John's feet jumped and heaved. Staggering, he shouted, "Get back in your seats. Strap yourselves in."

"Impact in sixty seconds," droned the computer.

"Come on, *come on*!" Emmie shouted. Knowing there was nothing else he could do, John threw himself into the seat Graal had left empty, pulling the harness over his shoulders. The red indicator line on the temperature gauge quivered at the very end of the dial. Emmie wrestled with the controls, fingers punching at the screen, trying to restart the spaceship's main engines.

"Impact in thirty seconds."

Steam and smoke streamed past the viewing window. Emmie wrenched desperately at the stick. The shuttle lurched to one side, setting off more screams. John's fingers clutched, white-knuckled, at the armrests, as the lip of a huge lava-spewing crater swept past the window.

"Impact in ten seconds."

A voice was shouting, "You can do it, Emmie!" With a jolt, John realized it was his own.

"I can't!" she screamed. "We're going to crash!"

CHAPTER 13

"Brace for impact!" Emmie roared.

The front of the shuttle lifted as the underside hit the planet's surface with a stomach-wrenching crash. Torn metal and rock spun past John's window. He gripped the arms of his seat and forced himself to breathe.

The shuttle bounced back into the air. Stabilizer jets screamed.

Emmie punched at the controls desperately as the ground hit the bottom of the shuttle again. This time the craft rolled wildly. John barely heard the screaming behind him; his eyes were fixed on Emmie. With a low shout, she lost her grip and was tossed backward. John grabbed her arm as she fell. "Hold on to me!" he bellowed in her ear.

In front, the viewing window was now a boiling mass of brown dust as the shuttle plowed through the surface of Zirion Beta. Barely slowing, it hit a larger rock. There was a loud explosion, then jagged cracks appeared across the window. Emmie tightened her grip around John's neck and buried her head in his shoulder. With the delicate cut-grass smell of her silver hair in his nostrils, John squeezed his own eyes closed and hung on to her for dear life.

Gouging a long scar into the planet's surface, the shuttle crashed and rolled across Zirion Beta. As John and Emmie clung to each other, they could hear the screams of their terrified classmates. Gradually — so gradually it was barely noticeable — the shuttle slowed. Using only the stabilizer jets, not designed for emergency landings, Emmie had somehow managed to steer the small craft onto a flat plain. The shuttle finally rolled to a halt.

"You did it, Emmie," John said as the shuttle exploded into cheers.

"*Brilliant,* Tarz!" shrieked Lishtig, leaning over the back of the seat. "That was *awesome.*"

"Is anyone hurt?" John shouted, releasing Emmie and standing up. "Everyone make sure the person next to them is okay."

Quickly, the students took stock. Except for Rantoo's gashed head, Kritta's four black eyes, and a few bruised tentacles, there were no serious injuries. Emmie, meanwhile, ran back up to the shuttle's control panel for a damage report.

"It's bad!" she shouted. "Even the stabilizer jets are gone now. The auxiliary scanners are still functioning, but that's about it. If they didn't build these ships to survive pretty much anything, we wouldn't even have those."

"Have you checked the scanner for other ships?" asked John, leaning over her.

"Doing that now," Emmie replied, jabbing at the screen. "No readings from any ships, but I am getting a beacon from a scientific station a few miles away."

She paused and turned back to face the ship with an unexpected grin on her face.

"We're in luck!" she yelled excitedly. "There's a Galactic Council science outpost just under two miles from here. It's unmanned, but Council protocol says every post must have an emergency shuttle. We can use it to fly back to Hyperspace High."

"Don't be a total fool, Tarz!" screamed a new voice. Tear-stained and deathly pale, Mordant stood. Glaring at her, he spat, "It may have escaped your stupid little head, but the Mega-Eruption is going to start any moment. If we go outside, we're dead."

"Uh, I hate to say it, but Mordant's got a point," growled Gobi-san-Art. "Aren't we better off waiting here for help to arrive? At least the shuttle will give us some protection."

"Thanks for getting us down, Emmie," said Rantoo through teeth clenched in pain. "But, just to check, you did send out a distress signal, didn't you?"

Emmie nodded. "Yes," she said. "Yes, of course I did."

"Well, then," said Mordant. "There you have it. That settles it. Hyperspace High will be sending out a rescue party right now. We'll be saved. We'll just stay here until it comes to get us."

John, meanwhile, had been doing some math in his head. "Hang on!" he called, holding up his hand. "The shuttle took four hours to get here, and Graal said there was just over two hours until the eruption began. That was about fifteen minutes ago."

At the mention of Doctor Graal's name, several students began muttering among themselves.

"She took the escape pod and left us to die," said Bareon, scowling. "Lorem should let her stay in it forever."

"No, she didn't!" screeched Mordant, sounding half-crazy with terror. "It *must* have been an accident. Doctor Graal would *never* —"

"For crying out loud, you really *are* a teacher's pet, aren't you?" Queelin shouted, the antennae on her head thrashing furiously. "Your precious Doctor Graal was only concerned with saving her own skin."

Although John agreed, arguing about it wasn't going to get them back to safety. Shaking his head, he continued, "What I'm saying is, there are just two hours left until the whole planet blows. A rescue mission won't have time to reach us. Not even the ship itself could change course and get here that quickly."

"I'm not getting off this shuttle!" yelled Mordant stubbornly. "G-Vez, check again for other ships in the area."

Emmie looked at him calmly. "There's nothing. John's right — if we stay here, we'll be caught in the Mega-Eruption. If we start walking now, there's a good chance we'll make it to the science outpost in time to get off the planet."

Several students called out their agreement.

"We *can* breathe out there, right?" asked Werril.

Emmie punched a few more panels. "Yes," she said a few seconds later. "The atmosphere's got enough oxygen to keep us alive. There are some poisonous gases, too, but we'll all be able to breathe it for at least a few hours."

"Don't listen to her!" Mordant shouted, his voice trembling with rage and fear. "She's the stupidest girl in school. Why would anyone listen to what she says? She'll get us all killed. We'll stay here. It's *safe* on the shuttle."

Unable to stop himself, John took a step toward the whining boy, fists clenched in rage. "Shut up, Mordant!" he shouted. "You're a coward, and your cowardice will get us all killed."

"There's no way this shuttle will withstand

an entire planet erupting around it," added Emmie loudly. "It's barely in one piece as it is."

"They're lying. Trying to be heroes," Mordant babbled, desperation in his voice. He looked around the shuttle for support from someone besides G-Vez. "Who put them in charge anyway? We should stay here and wait."

"I say we go," Lishtig cut in. "We're all okay to walk and there's nothing to carry. At a good pace we can easily cover a mile every fifteen minutes. That gives us plenty of time."

"I believe the boy's calculations are correct," buzzed G-Vez. "You could all easily —"

"Oh, shut up!" snapped Mordant.

The metal ball hovered silently.

"But what if a rescue party comes and can't find us?" Gobi asked.

"Lorem will get here in time. He would never let his students get hurt."

"You don't *know* that they'll get here in time, Werril. Emmie landed us safely; she can get us off the planet, too."

Suddenly everyone on the shuttle was shouting at the same time.

"*STOP!*"

There was a note of urgent authority in Kaal's thunderous shout that brought the shuttle to an immediate hush. Everyone turned to look at the green Derrilian.

Kaal pointed to the viewing window. "Zirion Beta's already made the decision for us," he said quietly. "The shuttle's sinking. We have to get off, and we have to get off *right now*."

John craned his neck to look through the window. Along the length of the shuttle, students gasped as they did the same. Kaal was right. Beneath the shuttle was the surface of a lava lake.

Under his feet, he felt a small movement as the craft sank a little farther.

For a second John stared through the viewing window, stunned. A second ago they had been safe, at least for the moment. Now they were being sucked down into a pool of deadly molten rock.

CHAPTER 14

There was no time left to argue — someone had to get things moving. With a tiny groan, John realized that the *someone* would have to be him.

Turning his head back to face the crowded shuttle, he shouted, "Okay, let's get out of here! Lishtig, you go first. Help people up to the roof. Kaal and I will stay down here and push from below." Looking around at the sea of frightened faces, John pressed a button by the door. It hissed open, letting a burst of boiling, stinking air onto the shuttle. "Let's go!" he shouted.

A few minutes later, Lishtig pulled at Gobi-san-Art's hand, his long purple hair blowing in the hot wind and sweat pouring down his face. "How many more?" he growled, straining to heave the massive bulk of Gobi upward.

John glanced past Kaal and down the aisle. "Eight," he replied. His own face was red from the planet's heat and the effort of giving his classmates a boost. Skin had already started to peel from his nose and cheeks. He looked out nervously. Slowly, the level of molten rock was rising against the side of the shuttle. Within a few minutes, it would begin pouring over the step. "We have to speed up!" he called to the others, trying to make his voice sound calm. "Mordant, you're next."

"I don't need any help," Mordant said, stepping forward and then cringing back again as the heat hit him. G-Vez buzzed around his head, one arm extending with a tiny fan at the end. It was useless in the intense heat but the droid still tried to cool its master.

"This is no time for pride!" John yelled back. "You're slowing us down."

With Gobi now helping, Lishtig pulled Mordant up and over the edge of the roof, feet scrabbling against the side of the shuttle. Quickly, Kaal helped the next student forward. Minutes later, only he and John were left inside.

"You go first," said the Derrilian.

"No —"

"What did you say to Mordant? Squabbling will only slow us down."

With Kaal boosting him from below, John scrambled up the roof of the sinking shuttle, where students huddled in the center, as far from the lava as possible. Immediately, he turned and held out a hand to his friend. Wings flapping in the hot air, Kaal quickly joined the group.

"So what now?" Kaal asked, looking around.

John spun around, his heart pounding. The shuttle was completely surrounded by lava. Then, through a haze of gas and heat, he spotted a spit of black rock that jutted out into the burning lake. Its tip was just two yards from the shuttle. "There!" he shouted, pointing. "We'll have to jump for it."

"No way," interrupted Mordant. "What if I slip?"

"Perhaps I could be of assistance, young master?"

"*Shut up*, you stupid piece of space junk," spat Talliver. "You can't carry me and I am *not* jumping."

"Pah, it's easy," said Lishtig. Without waiting, he ran to the side of the shuttle and launched himself into the air, arms whirling as he crossed the gap. With a hoot of triumph, he landed on all fours on the rocky ground, inches from the edge of the molten rock pool.

"Nice one, Lishtig!" John called over. "Who's going next?"

"I am *not* —" Mordant began again. His words choked off, as strong arms caught him around the chest and massive wings snapped at the air. "*Nooo!*" he screamed, feet thrashing as he was lifted over the side of the shuttle.

"Don't struggle," ordered Kaal as he flapped across to the shore. Dropping Mordant onto solid ground, Kaal landed beside him.

"You're *loving* this, aren't you?" he whispered angrily into Kaal's face. "Showing off in front of everyone and making me look pathetic."

Kaal beat his wings slowly and looked back toward the shuttle.

"I can take anyone who can't jump!" he called out.

John felt metal shift beneath his feet. Trying to keep a tight grip on his own fear, he shouted, "Anyone who thinks they can make it, come forward!"

Moments later, Queelin Temerate ran across the roof of the shuttle, only to come to a skidding halt a foot from the edge.

"I'm s-sorry," she stammered. "I th-thought I could do it, b-but —"

John saw the tears in her yellow eyes and felt her trembling when he put a reassuring hand on her shoulder. "It's okay," he said, pushing her gently toward the group waiting for Kaal to carry them across the lava.

Progress was slow. Aware that the minutes until the Mega-Eruption were ticking by, John did all he could to hurry the students, but

Queelin wasn't the only one to look down at the bubbling lava and change her mind. Meanwhile, the shuttle sank slowly into the lava. By the time John's turn finally came to make the leap, molten rock was oozing over the side of the roof.

He gulped. Pounding across the metal roof, he launched himself toward the narrow spit of land. As he jumped, a grinding rumble filled the air. Ahead of him the cone of a volcano belched smoke and sparks. John's feet touched the ground just as an earthquake began. Beneath him, the rock heaved, making his landing awkward. He stumbled, falling back toward the lava, hands flailing at empty air.

Kaal's hand grabbed him by the front of his jumpsuit and pulled him up.

"Whoa, that was close. Thanks, Kaal. You saved my life," John panted. He coughed while the ground groaned and shivered beneath him.

Kaal shrugged. "You owe me one. Buy me a drink at Ska's Café when we get back."

Skin raw from the heat, and hair smoking, John looked up into the Derrilian's face. Kaal was trying to sound cool, but his face showed his concern. John knew exactly how he felt. "I guess we'd better get moving," he said. "Which way?"

Emmie stepped forward, holding out what looked like two digital watches. "I took these from the shuttle," she explained. "Mini computers. They'll track the science outpost and act as translators. With the shuttle's computer gone, they'll make sure we can all still understand each other."

She snapped one onto her wrist and held the other out to John. He took it and put it on.

"We should have about an hour and forty minutes left," Emmie continued. "You keep an eye on the time. I'll lead the way."

With the ground trembling beneath their feet, the group of students trailed behind Emmie as she started out across the bleak plain. In the distance, volcanoes roared and spat. Tearing his eyes away from the vast cones, John stood to one side as the line of worried-looking students passed.

"If we all walk quickly, we'll be at the science outpost soon!" he called out.

"Thanks for stating the completely obvious," Mordant sneered from the back of the group.

"Save your breath for walking, Mordant."

Mordant immediately stumbled over a rock, falling to his knees in the dust with a curse. "Leave me alone!" he shouted, as John offered him a hand up. "I told you I don't need your help."

Shrugging, John left Mordant swearing at G-Vez. The little machine took its master's insults in silence and busied itself brushing dust from his clothes.

"Oww!" Mordant screeched. "You pinched me. That really hurt."

"A thousand apologies, young master," replied the drone, unperturbed.

Jogging ahead to catch up with Emmie, John asked, "How are we doing?"

"One point four seven miles," she said, glancing at her wrist computer's small screen. "That means we should get there with about fifteen minutes to spare, so long as there are no hold-ups."

"This is so stupid. We're going to die of heatstroke out here," whined a voice from behind John.

"Oh, for crying out loud. Stop *moaning*, Mordant!" came a shout.

John forced a smile to his heat-cracked

lips. "Maybe we *should* have let him stay on the shuttle," he said quietly.

Glancing back at the lava pool, Emmie shook her head. The small spaceship had disappeared beneath the surface. "He's just scared," she said simply. "We all are."

John just nodded, fighting down a fresh wave of panic, as the ground beneath his feet shuddered once more.

"I'm going to scout ahead from the air," Kaal interrupted, joining them.

"Be careful," Emmie and John said together.

"Will do."

John watched as his friend took to the sky on leathery wings, wishing he, too, had wings.

As he trudged across the forbidding landscape, the ground had begun to quake almost constantly. The planet's hot wind, heavy with chemical stench, blew dust into his eyes and ears. Before long, John was covered from head to foot. There was no choice but to keep walking.

* * *

"How are we doing now, Emmie?" John whispered, when his computer showed they had an hour left.

Emmie turned her dust-stained face toward his, lines creasing her forehead. "Too slow," she said. "We've still got at least a mile to go. At this pace, we're not going to make it."

"Good news!" shouted Kaal above them.

All the students looked up to where the Derrilian was circling. "I've seen the science outpost!" he called down. "The way is clear betwee—" The rest of Kaal's words were drowned by an eardrum-shredding shriek. A black shape swooped from the sky above, slashing at John's friend with outstretched talons. With a cry of fear, Kaal fell from the sky.

Through the swirling dust, John saw something that looked like a pterodactyl, its long snout — half-beak, half-muzzle — was lined with razor teeth. A bone crest jutted from the back of its head. The mottled skin of its wings ran from wingtip to its rear legs.

"Get down!" screamed Emmie, shoving John and sending him sprawling into the dust. John saw the creature swoop toward him. Claws snatched at the space where he had been standing seconds before. Then it swiped again, this time finding prey. Through horrified eyes, John watched as the creature's viciously hooked talons closed around Emmie. With a hideous shriek of victory, it flapped its wings and rose into the air — Emmie struggling in its claws.

CHAPTER 15

Scrambling to his knees, John stared aghast as the creature flapped away across the dusty landscape, Emmie writhing in its grip. He opened his lips to shout after her, but the wind that blew Emmie's screams across the plain filled his mouth with dust. All he could do was watch as the monster carried away his friend.

Get up, John. Do something, you useless idiot.

"Kaal," he croaked. He had to go after Emmie, and Kaal was the only one among them who could give chase. John ran through thick dust to where his friend had fallen. Dropping down to his side, he shook the Derrilian by the shoulder. "Kaal, are you hurt?"

Groaning, Kaal sat up, rubbing his ribs with one hand. "What was *that*?" he choked, flexing his wings and checking them for damage. "It came out of nowhere."

"Doesn't matter what it was. It got Emmie," John told him. "We have to go after it. Can you fly?"

Kaal was already on his feet, wings beating strong. There was a small tear in the leathery skin, but he paid it no attention. "Get on," he answered grimly, turning so that John could climb onto his broad back.

Mordant staggered toward them across the shaking ground. "What's this?" he demanded. "You're leaving? What about us?"

John's hands were already on Kaal's

shoulders. Turning toward Mordant, unable to hide his scorn at the boy's selfishness, he took the mini computer from his wrist and hurled it at the half-Gargon's chest.

"That will lead you straight to the science outpost," he replied angrily. "If the Mega-Eruption begins before we get back, then you'll just have to leave without us."

"But —"

John, however, had finished with Mordant. He jumped up, gripped the sides of Kaal's torso with his knees and pointed over his shoulder. "*Go.* It went toward the volcano with the half-collapsed crater. There." The pterodactyl creature was now just a black dot against the brown sky.

John's stomach lurched as his friend leaped upward. For a moment, Kaal seemed to struggle to say aloft — his great wings pounded, swirling dust — but as he adjusted to carrying a passenger, they began climbing into the sky.

"Hurry up!" John yelled down to the others, and then scanned the horizon for the tiny speck that carried Emmie away from them. Shielding his eyes, he frowned and squinted his eyes against the constantly blowing dust.

Below, the rumbling beneath the planet's surface increased. In the distance, the crater of another volcano lit up like a giant firework, shooting sparks and great gobs of white-hot rock into the sky. John could feel his friend's muscles heaving as the Derrilian pushed himself to the limits of his strength.

"Higher. Need . . . more . . . height . . ." Kaal grunted. Then, *"Husharg . . . n'quar . . . taskit."*

John tore his eyes from the alien creature carrying Emmie and stared at his friend, wondering why he had started speaking gibberish. "What?" he shouted. "I don't understand."

Kaal glanced back over his shoulder, a frown crossing his green face. "*Cartikka churg?*" he shouted back.

"Why are you speaking like —" John began. Understanding dawned. They were beyond the range of the computers. He was hearing untranslated Derrilian, and Kaal was hearing English.

"*Cartikka?*" Kaal repeated, looking back at John.

In reply, John tapped his wrist. "No computer!" he shouted.

Kaal's reply turned into a cough, as a sudden rain of ash began falling; the cough turned into a yelp of pain, as a falling ember punched another hole through his wing. John could see nothing through the falling ash.

"Kaal! *Kaal?* You okay?" he panted.

Kaal didn't respond, but his wings kept beating. Seconds later, they burst free of the ash. The creature was still ahead of them.

"We're gaining on it!" John yelled, hoping Kaal would hear the excited tone of his voice, even if he couldn't understand the words. Now he could make out Emmie's limp body clutched in its talons. As John watched, the beast swerved off its course, making for the smoking cone of a smaller volcano.

Gulping down the terrifying thought that Emmie might already be dead, John pointed over his friend's shoulder again and yelled, "Veer right!" John leaned into the turn, as Kaal swooped to the right.

Minutes ticked by as they followed the fleeing creature into a maze of volcanoes. Streams of fire poured from craters, joining to become a vast river of lava running along a valley floor. John gritted his teeth, wanting to tell Kaal to hurry but knowing that his friend was already straining every muscle. Instead, he tried to count the minutes, calculating how long they had left before the planet exploded into one vast eruption.

Suddenly, the monster dived with a flick of its wings. For a second, it hovered over the rim of a volcano before dropping Emmie. John winced as her body smashed onto rock on the lip of the crater and rolled down the slope. Landing on the rim just above its prey, the creature's razor teeth gnashed at the air. A talon reached out and claimed its prize. Spreading its wings and lifting its long muzzle, it screeched in triumph and hunger.

In John's mind, terror turned to rage — an eruption as fiery as any of the volcanoes around them. "*KAAL!*" he screamed. "It's going to kill her."

Kaal had already seen. His wings swept back. Now John understood why his friend had been so determined to gain height. Wind whipped his hair back from his face as they fell toward the beast; gravity gave them speed. Kaal's wings beat in a fury that matched John's white-hot anger. Faster and faster they hurtled toward the creature.

It bent down to begin tearing at Emmie.

John bellowed a ferocious challenge.

Confused, the beast looked up from its prey. Just then, John and Kaal hit it full in the chest. The creature screamed as it fell backward into the volcano, its wings thrashing as John's fingers closed around its throat. At the same time, Kaal's powerful hands gripped the creature's wing, breaking bones like twigs.

Whirling, it howled in agony, talons clawing at thin air, one wing flapping uselessly. It twisted, trying to free itself from its attackers. John's fingers tightened around the creature's throat, barely noticing as he was thrown from Kaal's back by the beast's frenzied convulsions.

"JOHN!"

With a start, John realized that he could understand Kaal again. Emmie's computer must still be working. But at the same time, he also realized that he was falling fast.

Crippled and shrieking, the beast was spiraling down into the smoky-hot depths of the volcano, carrying John with it. Releasing his grip, John looked up desperately. Above was a circle of light that made up the rim of the volcano. For half a second, John tumbled, clutching at nothing but smoke. A scream formed on his cracked lips.

But suddenly a hand reached though the smoke and grabbed his wrist. John gripped it. With a clap of beating wings, his descent came to a sudden stop. Green arms reached out for him.

John glanced down, once, while Kaal pulled him from the blasting heat of the volcano's crater. The creature had disappeared, but the depths below thundered and groaned. The Mega-Eruption was very close.

Bursting out of the smoke, John and Kaal dropped to the ground, coughing. Their feet started small landslides of pebbles as they slipped down the slope to Emmie. John leant over her still body, his face close to her mouth, feeling her shallow breathing with a wave of relief that brought tears to his eyes.

"She's alive!" he shouted.

"Broken arm," replied Kaal.

John looked down. Emmie's arm was twisted at a stomach-churning angle. Gently, he unclipped the mini computer that was fastened to her wrist and snapped it onto his own.

"John? Kaal?" Emmie's eyes fluttered open.

"It's okay, it's okay!" John yelled above the rumbling. "We're going to get you out of here."

Emmie slipped out of consciousness again. Worried, John looked up into Kaal's face. "You *can* carry us both, can't you?"

"*No choice.*" John could barely hear the words — the roar of the volcano was deafening — but he understood Kaal's shrug.

A few feet away, a crack opened in the rock. Fresh smoke billowed from the summit, carrying with it the first sparks of eruption.

John glanced down at the computer. With horror, he saw that there was little more than half an hour left before the Mega-Eruption turned Zirion Beta into a ball of fire. It would take almost twenty minutes to get back to where they had started, and this time Kaal would be carrying two people.

"Come *on!*" Kaal's roar interrupted his thoughts. The Derrilian had picked Emmie up and was holding her protectively to his chest.

John swung himself, once again, onto his friend's broad back.

As Kaal's wings stretched out, an enormous boom rocked the volcano and hunks of molten rock began shooting into the sky.

CHAPTER 16

On a thunderous storm of burning sparks, Kaal swept into the sky, John clinging to his back, Emmie clutched in his arms.

The heat was intense. John noticed more small holes in his friend's wings, the edges singed and burned. His own skin was raw and blistering in places. Part of him wanted to squeeze his eyes closed and just hang on, but there was still a slim chance they could beat the Mega-Eruption and get off the planet. Kaal still needed his help.

On his wrist computer, a green light was flashing. *The science outpost*, John thought. A red light tracked their own position. Kaal was heading back the way they had come, but it wasn't the shortest route. Yelling to make himself heard, John hung over his friend's neck and pointed out a new course. "Can you make it?" he asked, gasping.

"Think so," Kaal grunted through teeth clenched with effort. "Heat good. Uplift."

John frowned, puzzling over the words before he understood what Kaal had meant. The Derrilian was riding the super-heated air rising from lava below. It was pushing them higher, keeping them aloft. Kaal wasn't so much flying now as he was controlling a long glide, his wings providing direction and extra speed. Even carrying the extra weight of Emmie, they were making faster progress than before.

But fast enough? John wondered.

All around, more volcanoes were beginning to explode. The air was dangerously hot. Fine hairs on John's arms were crisping. Every lungful of air he took was painful.

He could feel muscles beneath his hands begin twitching with fatigue. Even with the air currents helping, Kaal was tiring fast. "Getting closer!" John yelled. "Nearly there."

His heart sank as he glanced down at the computer again. Encouraging words dried on his lips. They were still a mile away from the science outpost, and volcano after volcano was now igniting as the Mega-Eruption spread across Zirion Beta.

An ember hit John in the chest, instantly burning its way through his light jumpsuit, sizzling his skin. He bit down on the cry of agony that escaped his lips, knowing that Kaal and Emmie were in far worse pain. With every passing second, the air was filled with the noise of fresh explosions. Below, the planet's surface buckled and tore like paper.

And still, Kaal flew on. Wings tattered and torn, dripping sweat from exertion and heat, the Derrilian powered his way through the burning air.

"There!" bellowed John at last, pointing ahead wildly. Half-hidden by dust, ash, and falling cinders, a collection of low, squat buildings stood out against the rugged horizon.

Kaal corrected his course and dived for it, his wings driving them forward in one last, mighty effort.

"John! Kaal! Over here!"

John's head snapped around, his heart pumping, as Kaal skidded to a halt in the dust. Lishtig hung from the door of a shuttle, waving frantically. Jumping from his friend's back, John caught Kaal around the waist as his friend dropped to his knees in exhaustion. Gently, he took Emmie from Kaal's arms. Relieved of her slight weight, Kaal managed to struggle to his feet again. Together, they staggered the last few feet to the steps of the shuttle.

"Can Tarz fly us out of here?" Lishtig asked as they climbed aboard.

John shook his head. "No." Then he stopped dead at the front of the shuttle, eyes widening. "What's going on here?"

A few rows back, Mordant was struggling in his seat, hissing and scowling. Crossing his chest and tied behind him were his own long black tentacles. Gobi-san-Art loomed over him, trying to swat away the screeching G-Vez.

"We got here ten minutes ago," Lishtig explained. "Mordant tried to take off immediately. He said you were already dead and wouldn't be coming back."

"The coward wanted to save his own skin and leave you to die," added Rantoo. "Just like Graal."

"Must be the Gargon genes," said Werril.

"Uh . . . can we go now?" piped Bareon nervously from the back of the shuttle. "You know, Mega-Eruption and everything."

Carefully, John settled Emmie in a seat at the front that had been left free. Trying not to move her mangled arm, he tightened a harness around her. Trembling from exhaustion, Kaal fell into the seat behind her.

"What are we waiting for?" John shouted to Lishtig over his shoulder. "Tell the shuttle computer to get us out of here."

"This isn't a Hyperspace High shuttle, John," Lishtig replied, moving aside so that

John could get a clear view of the pilot's seat. "Old technology. Never supposed to be used. The Council wouldn't waste a new shuttle with autopilot on a science outpost."

"Get in the pilot's seat, John," said a small voice. "I'll help you."

Emmie was awake. John looked down into navy-blue eyes that were filled with pain — and determination.

"*Me?*" he said. "Why me? What about Kaal? Or Lishtig? Why not Gobi?"

In reply, Kaal slumped in his seat, groaning. John could tell that his friend was in no shape to fly the shuttle.

"Not me," said Lishtig. "Have you seen my takeoffs?"

"You do it, John," said Gobi. "You've been having extra lessons."

"Just hurry up and *get us out of here?*" screeched

Mordant. "Come on! Before the whole planet explodes!"

Throwing himself into the pilot's seat and fastening the harness, John looked over the controls.

"They should be similar to the ones on the t-darts," Emmie said behind him. "Close and lock, then start the engines."

John looked down. Sure enough, there was a locking lever by his feet, just like on the small spaceships he had flown around the hangar. He pulled it and the door hissed closed. Looking to the right of the control panel, he found the "Start Engines" panel and stabbed at it with his finger.

The shuttle rocked, almost toppling, as another massive earthquake shook the ground. Through the windshield, he saw the ground split apart in a great jagged gash that raced toward the shuttle. Nearby science outpost buildings collapsed, throwing more dust into the air. The rear of the shuttle dropped into the newly formed ravine with awful suddenness.

Mordant began screaming hysterically, twisting in his seat. The sound was quickly cut off when Gobi slapped one of his massive hands across Mordant's wailing mouth. Lishtig managed to grab the equally crazed G-Vez and stuffed it into a bag.

Every student on the shuttle held their breath.

"Now, grip the control stick firmly, power up, and release," Emmie continued, as if nothing had happened.

His hand shaking, John gripped the stick. All the terrible takeoffs he had ever made came back to him at once. And those had been on the hangar deck of Hyperspace High, not on a convulsing planet that was about to explode any second.

I can't do this.

"You can do this," Emmie said gently, as if reading his mind. "Power up now."

John's hand reached for another panel. He punched the power up to three. The shuttle began to vibrate softly.

"Now release and pull the nose up gently."

John flicked the switch on the control stick. The shuttle began to drag itself out of the gaping chasm. "Nose up," said Emmie sharply.

Fighting down panic, John pulled back on the control stick, as Sergeant Jegger had taught him — firmly but smoothly. The front of the shuttle rose. Inch by inch, the little spaceship dragged itself from the hole, thrumming with power. With a final lurch and a squeak of metal, it came free and started climbing slowly. John heard dull thuds and clangs as embers rattled against it.

"Now point her at the sky and punch the power up to max," Emmie said, panting through her pain. "Get us out of here, John."

John's fingers were reaching for the panel before she had even finished. Every student was thrown back in their seat as he accelerated hard. Fighting against the G-force, his hand reached out and hit "Acceleration Boost" for good measure.

Gripping the control stick, John allowed the force to push him back. Already the viewing screen was coated with dust. All he could do now was keep the shuttle pointed in the right direction and hope they weren't hit by anything larger than a cinder.

The shuttle plowed into the sky.

John squeezed his eyes shut.

"John. John . . . *Riley*. It's okay. We made it. Slow her down now." Emmie's voice again.

A small matter-of-fact part of John's mind told him that the crushing weight of the gravitational force on his chest had gone. The rain of cinders had stopped.

They were in space. Safe.

John blinked. He turned, looking directly into Emmie's shining eyes. She smiled at him. Behind her, Kaal managed to raise a hand in salute. "Nice flying," he said quietly.

"Woo-hoo! Doctor Slobber was right about one thing. That is freaking *spectacular*."

John craned his head round the back of his seat. Lishtig was kneeling, staring through the viewing window. Beyond him, Zirion Beta burst into fire. Every volcano erupted at once, cascading white-hot lava. Great fountains of white, red, and gold spewed, before crashing back to cover the entire planet in a sea of molten rock. Across the atmosphere, clouds of sparks danced in continent-sized swirls of glittering light.

Students crowded in around Lishtig, eyes wide in awe as they watched.

Soon, John could no longer see. Too many students were in the way. He tore his eyes away from the scene with only a tiny pang of regret. He'd already seen enough volcanoes erupt that day to last a lifetime.

Instead, he reached out to power down and slow the shuttle's velocity. As he touched the screen, a speaker on the control panel crackled and burst into life. "Shuttle just departed from Zirion Beta. *Come in.* Repeat: Shuttle departing Zirion Beta. *Report.*"

Painfully, a grin spread across John's cracked and blistered face. "Hello, Zepp," he croaked.

CHAPTER 17

At the sound of Zepp's voice, the shuttle exploded with cheers.

"John. John. *JOHN!*" chanted Lishtig, kicking away from his seat and floating forward in zero gravity to slap John on the back. The rest of the students rushed to join him.

"You should get the Galactic Medal of Outstanding Awesomeness," squealed Queelin, throwing her pale-blue arms around John's neck. "That was so amazing, John! Oh, I can't believe it!"

"We'll get Lorem to put up a statue of you in the Center."

"You saved our lives."

"Way to go, John."

Only Mordant was silent. Still tied to his seat, he scowled furiously.

Blushing, John held up his hands for quiet. Zepp was still speaking, drowned out by the cheering. "Hey!" John bellowed. "It's Kaal and Emmie you should be thanking, but shut up and listen."

"I was just saying," said Zepp, "that thanks to whomever sent out the distress call, the ship is on its way at maximum speed. Stand by, Hyperspace High is coming to get you. Estimated time of arrival four minutes and twenty-six seconds. We are all *very* relieved to hear your voices."

More cheering followed. John found himself

unclipped from his harness and tossed from hand to fin to claw to hand along the length of the jubilant shuttle.

"Put me down!" he yelled. The familiar shape of Hyperspace High appeared outside the viewing window. "I still have to land this thing."

"Taken care of," said Sergeant Jegger's voice through the speaker. "We're patching into the shuttle's systems now. You've done enough for one day, cadet. I'll bring this bird in."

Once the ship had docked, John's classmates hurried through the door onto Hyperspace High's hangar deck.

John waited for the crowd to die down before untying Mordant's tentacles. His reward was a look of pure poison.

"You may think you're the big hero now," Mordant spat, "but tomorrow you'll be back on your own pathetic little world. In a week no one here is going to even remember you."

As John's hands curled into fists, a voice behind him said, "I'll remember him."

"Me, too."

John relaxed as he turned to look over each shoulder. On one side, Kaal was on his feet, swaying but upright. On the other stood Emmie, cradling her broken arm. With a thin smile, John folded his own arms and said, "Guess you're wrong again, Mordant. But you must be getting used to it by now."

Without another word, Mordant stalked off the shuttle.

"Thanks," John said, smiling at his friends. "Now, come on. Let's get you both some medical attention."

"Ha," said Kaal with a grin as they walked down the aisle. "A Derrilian isn't a Derrilian until they have a few scars. I'm going to be telling stories about these for years."

"Don't forget to mention me."

"Believe me, my grandchildren will know all about the incredibly stupid human their granddad had to pull out of a volcano."

John grinned at his roommate.

By the time John and Kaal helped Emmie out of the shuttle door, the three of them were choking with laughter, despite their wounds. They stopped abruptly when they saw the headmaster waiting for them. Behind him was every student and teacher on Hyperspace High. The entire ship had come down to see the first years safely returned. John caught Sergeant Jegger's eye as his gaze swept across the crowd. The flight teacher stood at attention and nodded approvingly to him and then to Emmie.

The last shred of laughter died on John's

lips as he spotted Doctor Graal standing among the teachers, a worried look on her usually stern face.

Noticing where John was glaring, Lorem stepped forward. "We picked up the escape pod en route," he said, softly. Changing the subject, he tilted his head and continued in a louder voice, "John, Kaal, Emmie. I am already hearing amazing things about the three of you. Perhaps, however, you would be so kind as to tell me what happened yourselves."

"All in good time, Headmaster," interrupted a high-pitched voice. John had never seen the woman with metallic-looking skin and enormous black eyes who stepped forward. But from her crisp, white uniform — and the fact that she was walking alongside a floating hover-stretcher — he guessed that she was the ship's doctor. "I *must* take care of them first."

"Of course, Doctor Kasaria," replied Lorem, stepping back to let her pass. "How remiss of me."

"Only Emmie and Kaal need a doctor," John said quickly. "I'm all right."

"Multiple first- and second-degree burns," replied Doctor Kasaria briskly, looking him up and down. "They will need treating as soon as possible."

She switched her attention to Emmie. "Hmmm," she said. "Impacted fracture *and* a dislocated shoulder. We'll take care of you first. Please lie down," she said, pointing to the hover-stretcher.

Emmie started to protest.

"I'm afraid I will have to insist," said the doctor firmly.

"It's best not to argue with Doctor Kasaria, Emmie," the headmaster cut in. "However, doctor, perhaps you could spare us John Riley and Kaal for a few moments. I will have them delivered straight to the medical center as soon as possible."

"Very well, Headmaster," said Kasaria reluctantly, pushing Emmie toward the TravelTube. "Please make sure it *is* only a few moments."

"Well . . . John? Kaal?" Lorem said, as Emmie was whisked away.

John and Kaal looked at each other. Kaal nodded at John to go ahead.

"It started when the shuttle was hit by asteroids. That was when Doctor Graal abandoned us," said John bluntly, in a voice loud enough to be heard by every student. "She forced her way past everyone, climbed into the escape pod, and blasted away before anyone else had a chance to get in with her."

A shocked gasp ran around the hangar deck, followed by Doctor Graal's voice. "How *dare* you! Headmaster, I must protest. I have already explained what happened. It was a simple accident."

"When we picked up Doctor Graal, she explained that she was preparing the pod for launch when she pressed the wrong panel," said Lorem evenly. "She was as horrified as anyone else when the pod launched."

"I *told* you," Mordant Talliver spat. "It *was* an accident."

It was John's turn to gasp. "That's not what happened," he choked, ignoring Talliver. "She was pushing everyone aside in her hurry to escape."

"I was trying to get to the pod as quickly as possible," Graal squelched forward on slimy tentacles, her voice blubbering with outrage.

"*That* is true. As you know, Headmaster, all teachers are trained for emergency situations and I didn't want to waste a second. Really, I shouldn't have to be cross-examined in front of the whole school by a *student*, let alone a primitive who shouldn't be on board anyway."

"But —" John began.

Lorem raised a hand, stopping him before he could call the teacher a liar in front of the whole school. "I understand how the situation must have looked, John Riley," he said firmly. "But Doctor Graal is a respected teacher, and I will take her word as the truth. That is, unless you have any proof to back up your accusation?" Lorem looked into his eyes searchingly.

John returned the gaze, reading a warning in Lorem's eyes. Mouth set in a grim line, he shook his head. "No," he said at last. "I don't have any proof, but —"

"Then perhaps you could proceed with your story," said the headmaster more kindly.

Let it go, said a small voice in John's mind. *It's your word against hers.*

John shook his head and continued, slowly at first, but with increasing speed as he warmed to his tale. Here and there, Kaal interrupted, supplying the headmaster with details that John had skipped over. As the story progressed, other students began to chip in, too.

"It seems to me, John Riley," said the headmaster, as John finished, "that everyone on board owes you — and Kaal and Emmie — a debt of gratitude."

Over Lorem's shoulder, John saw Doctor Graal's mouth twist into a sneer. Deciding to ignore her, he looked back at the headmaster.

"Well . . . everyone kind of worked together," he said, his cheeks feeling hot from embarrassment as well as from his burns. "It wasn't just us three."

"Nevertheless," the headmaster said, "it is plain from what you have said, and from what your classmates have told me, that the three of you acted with courage, showing loyalty to your fellow students and great leadership. Everyone at Hyperspace High is proud of you three."

Still blushing, John looked down. "No problem, sir," he mumbled.

"And now," Lorem continued with a smile. "I've already kept you too long. Those burns look painful and I made Doctor Kasaria a promise."

"I'm fine. Honestly. I just need to get to bed," Kaal said, yawning. "I've never been so exhausted."

"Let the doctor take a look at you," replied Lorem sympathetically. "It won't take long and her objections will almost certainly give *me* severe ear damage if you do not."

Despite Lorem's promise, however, the doctor was very thorough. It was another two hours before John and Kaal said goodbye to Emmie and left the medical bay. Clean and smothered with a sticky lotion that Doctor Kasaria promised would heal their burns quickly, they both climbed into bed without a word.

"Anyone for some music?" Zepp's voice asked.

The only reply was a snore like a rumbling volcano from Kaal's bed pod.

CHAPTER 18

An insistent chiming sound rang in John's ears, quickly becoming part of his dream. Mumbling, "Not today, thank you. Please come back tomorrow," he pulled the covers tight around his head.

"John. Kaal. You have a visitor."

That was a familiar voice. In his sleep John frowned, then sat bolt upright. "Wha—? *What? What* is it, Zepp?"

"You have a visitor," said the computer patiently. "Should I open the door?"

"Yes, yes of course. Unless it's Doctor Graal. Or Talliver . . . um . . . who is it?" John babbled as the door hissed open.

"It's me," said Emmie Tarz, marching into the room. "I've been outside for ages and . . . *Whoa!* Does your hair always look like that in the morning?"

"And hello to you, too," John muttered, running a hand through the blond mess on his head.

Kaal's screen slid back. With a rustle of wings, he sat up in bed, yawning. "What's the fuss about?"

"Kaal, don't you think John's hair makes him look like a Batrav sea anemone?"

"Thanks, Emmie," John cut in before Kaal could answer. He looked her up and down. She looked clean and fresh, her own hair a glossy, sparkling mane and her skin glowing. Her arm, however, was in a sling. "What are you doing here?" he continued. "Not that it isn't great to see you and everything, but shouldn't you be in the medical center?"

Emmie sat gracefully on the arm of a sofa, swinging one leg. The smile vanished from her face, quickly replaced with a look of sadness. "Lorem just came to visit me," she said. "He was on his way here to tell you that we're close to Earth. I told him I'd bring the message myself. I thought we could all have breakfast together one last time on the way to the hangar deck. You'll be leaving in just over an hour."

The color drained from John's face. He'd slept through his last hours on Hyperspace High. All the things he'd planned to do — the game of Zero-G war, the big feast with Emmie and Kaal, the evening at Ska's Café, the last t-dart flight — would now never happen.

"Oh. Okay," he managed to say. "Breakfast. Good idea. I'll get dressed."

"Me, too," said Kaal, already springing out of bed.

"I'll be waiting outside," said Emmie, walking to the door. "Hurry, we don't have long."

Without thinking, John reached for one of the silver and red school outfits in his locker. "I'm sorry, but you cannot wear that," Zepp's voice said gently. "You can only take what you came with. Headmaster's orders. If you carry any proof of your stay here to Earth, the Galactic Council will be furious."

"I see," said John sadly, reaching for his old backpack. "So no last photo with Kaal and Emmie, either, then?"

The computer paused, then whispered, "I may be able to bend the rules, as long as you promise never to show anyone."

"Done," said John. At least he would have something to remember his friends by.

"And there's something in your bag from me," the computer continued. "It's Earth technology; no one will ever notice."

John peered into the backpack. Resting on top of his neatly pressed clothes was the silver sheen of a plain compact disc.

"Just a few tunes," said Zepp. "I hope you like it."

"It's awesome," whispered John. "I'll think of you whenever I play it."

"Come on," said Kaal softly. "Emmie's waiting."

John ducked into the bathroom quickly, sticking his head under the tap. Brushing his teeth quickly, he looked into the mirror. His eyes widened. The night before, his face had been a mass of blisters and raw skin. Now it was completely smooth, as if nothing had happened. He checked his chest where the cinder had burned him. There was only healthy skin, slightly pink but otherwise unmarked. *No proof*, he thought. *Not even a scar.*

Zepp provided a delicious breakfast. None of them had eaten since taking a few bites of their packed lunches the day before and they all ate hungrily, trying to fit in as much talk as they could around the mouthfuls of food. John couldn't help feeling faintly ill as he watched Kaal's sharp teeth tearing at mouthfuls of his favorite food. It still seemed like skinned worms. *At least I'll never have to eat alien food again*, he thought.

The meal was over too quickly. John tried to keep up with Kaal and Emmie's jokes, and he forced himself to smile, but there was sadness beneath the chatter. Tears pricked his eyes when he found a photograph beneath his plate: John and Kaal and Emmie laughing together outside the dormitory. Emmie had just made another joke about his hair. John had no idea how Zepp had taken it, but he slipped it into his backpack gratefully.

Swallowing a mouthful of juice, John swung his backpack over his shoulder and said goodbye to Lishtig, Gobi, and a few other students who had rushed down to the cafeteria. Word had spread that he was leaving.

"Galva-coated Dumpod candy," said Lishtig, pressing a bag into John's hand.

"Thanks, but I'm not allowed to take anything. The Galactic Council —"

"Who cares what the Galactic Council thinks?" Lishtig said, winking.

John pocketed the candy.

* * *

"Good morning, John Riley. I am glad to see you are punctual this time."

As he walked out of the TravelTube, John was surprised to see Ms. Vartexia waiting by the shuttle, ThinScreen in hand and wearing her full Earth disguise.

"I will be delivering you to . . . where is it?" She checked her screen. "Oh, yes. Wortham Court School. How could I forget. It's all been worked out. You have made a full recovery from the measles, and as your aunt — that's me — happened to be traveling close to the school, she is dropping you off. After that, I will pick up Prince Clo-Ra-Ta."

"I see," said John, wondering what the people at Wortham Court would make of his bizarre aunt. "Well, at least they won't be throwing me

272

out of an airlock when I arrive, I guess. Right? Ha."

"Humor," said Ms. Vartexia, nodding as if a great secret had been revealed to her. "I have been studying it. Very . . . what's the word? . . . Oh, yes, *funny*. Ha-ha. Please board the shuttle."

"Just one second." John turned to Emmie and Kaal. "I guess this is goodbye, then."

"Wide skies, John Riley," said Kaal, laying a hand on John's shoulder. "If you are ever near Derril, come flying with me. No volcanoes."

"I will," John replied, knowing he would almost certainly never leave Earth again. "I'd say come visit me, but you'd have to get a really, really good disguise."

"Goodbye, John. I'll miss you," said Emmie, throwing her good arm around him and burying her face in his neck.

He felt tears on his shoulder. "I'll miss you,

too, Emmie," he said, feeling tears welling up in his own eyes. "Keep an eye on Kaal. Make sure he doesn't get into too much trouble with Talliver."

"Our launch window will soon be closing," said Ms. Vartexia sternly. "Please board the shuttle."

John raised a hand to his friends in salute. Then he turned away.

"Takeoff in eighteen seconds," said Ms. Vartexia, as she climbed up after him. "John, it will be a much longer trip this time. About three hours. The ship's computer tells me to say that you had better eat the Galva-coated Dumpod candy you have in your pocket before we arrive."

John pushed his backpack into an overhead locker and sank into a seat. Looking down, he clipped his harness on and lifted his head just in time to see a flashing ball of energy zip through the door.

"Good morning," said Lorem, as the ball twinkled into the shape of an old man.

"Good morning, Headmaster," said Ms. Vartexia briskly. "We were just leaving. Perfectly on time."

"I am sorry to delay you, but if I could just have a word with your passenger, I will keep it as quick as possible," Lorem replied, skin still twinkling. "And if you wouldn't mind waiting outside . . ."

"Of course," the Elvian replied politely but with a note in her voice that seemed to say, "If we're late, it won't be *my* fault." Laying her ThinScreen on an empty seat, she stepped down from the shuttle. The door closed behind her.

Lorem sat down across from John and looked into his eyes. Once again, John had the unsettling feeling that the headmaster knew *everything.* "I wanted to thank you again for your bravery on Zirion Beta," Lorem said quietly.

"Did you know that was going to happen?" John blurted. "Was that the adventure you saw?"

Lorem smiled. "As I told you," he said slowly, "the future is not always clear." John opened his mouth to ask another question, but Lorem held up one finger. "But I knew that you would play an important part in saving the lives of your classmates, and *that* would lead us to another important moment."

"What moment?" asked John, frowning.

"*This* moment," Lorem answered gravely. Seeing John's look of confusion, he smiled and continued. "Hyperspace High students are very carefully selected, John Riley. *Very* carefully selected. Some of them are the brightest scientific minds their worlds have to offer, some talented in music or art. Others have different qualities."

"I know. It's a great honor to be invited to join the school." John frowned again, wondering why Lorem was telling him this.

"If I were a mind reader, I would say that, once again, you are wondering why I am telling you this."

"Um . . . yes," John mumbled.

"Hyperspace High looks for many things in its students," Lorem explained. "And one of those things is courage. You showed exceptional bravery on Zirion Beta, John Riley."

"Thank you, sir," said John. "I'll always remember you said that."

"You don't understand me," said Lorem, his eyes bright. "I am offering you a place at Hyperspace High. A permanent place. That is, if you want it."

John's mouth fell open. "You mean *stay*? Not go back to Earth?" he said.

"Not now, no. You would, of course, go back at the end of the semester, but return here after the holidays. If you choose to stay, it will mean some bother with the Galactic Council and we will have to keep your parents in the dark, but . . ."

"Yes!" John's shout cut the headmaster off mid-sentence. "Yes, yes, yes. I would *love* it!" A grin spread across his face. A grin so wide, it was already making his face ache.

"Even without looking into the future, I thought you might say that," Lorem said, with a fresh smile of his own. "Your clothes are still in your room. I'm sure you'll want to continue sharing with Kaal, of course. Clo-Ra-Ta will have to take a dormitory to himself, but Martians enjoy their privacy."

John was already unfastening his harness. "So, I can get off this shuttle, then?" he asked.

"There's one other thing," said Lorem quietly, leaning over to pick up Ms. Vartexia's ThinScreen. "A few minutes ago, your parents called Wortham Court. That's why I was a little late getting here."

Panic crossed John's face. Had his mom and dad discovered he wasn't in England at boarding school after all?

"Don't worry, Zepp intercepted the call. I spoke to your mother myself. A highly intelligent human, if I may say so. I wish I'd had her as a student . . . but I'm losing the point. She and your father are extremely worried about you. They believe you are unhappy at your new school and phoned to say they will be arriving later today to take you home."

John groaned, holding his head in his hands

as he remembered the last conversation he had had with his mom and dad.

"I told them you were in a class and would call back. Before you make your final decision, I would like you to speak with them," said Lorem, tapping the ThinScreen. "Zepp, would you be so kind as to connect us?"

"Certainly, Headmaster," said Zepp's voice. "Patched into the Internet and ready."

The ThinScreen showed the Skype homepage.

John clicked the "call" button.

John's parents must have been sitting by the computer waiting for the call. His mom answered immediately. His dad was standing behind her, jangling car keys.

"John," she said, before he could get a word in. "Your dad and I have been talking. We're not going to ask you to stay at boarding school if you're unhappy. We'll be there to pick you up in a few hours —"

"Mom, *stop!*" John interrupted. "I love it here at . . . uh . . . Wortham Court."

His mother blinked, looking confused. "Oh. But you seemed so gloomy."

"It took me a while to get used to it, but I'm having the best time now," John replied quickly. "I'm sorry I made you worry, but I really want to stay."

"Are you sure?" asked his dad. He leaned over John's mom's shoulder, a frown creasing his forehead.

"*Positive*, Dad," John said. He laughed. "I've got some great friends, and we had an *awesome* field trip. It's the best school *ever.*"

His dad's face, too, broke into a grin. "You're just saying that because you know I'll thrash you at Doom Hammer as soon as you get back."

"Ha!" John laughed. "Wait until the break. I'll make you eat those words."

"Well, if you're sure," his mom cut in with a smile of her own. "I'll call the headmaster and tell him we won't be coming after all."

"Thanks, Mom. Thanks, Dad. I'll call you in a few days. Gotta go now, some friends are waiting for me."

"Thank you, sir," John said breathlessly as the call ended. "This is the greatest . . ."

"Headmaster. There is a call coming through from Earth," Zepp interrupted.

"Put it through, Zepp," replied Lorem, motioning to John that he could leave.

As he ran for the shuttle door, John heard Lorem saying, "Ah, Mrs. Riley . . . yes. Wonderful. I'm so pleased John will be staying. He's an excellent student with so much potential."

There was no time to listen. Kaal and

Emmie were standing by the TravelTube. The door was just hissing open. Sprinting across the deck, John shouted their names. Together, they spun around, looking bewildered as he charged up to them.

"Did you forget something?" Kaal asked. "Ms. Vartexia is going to —"

"No. I'm not leaving. I'm staying."

"What are you talking about, John?" Emmie said. "You can't stay. Lorem will . . . you *have* to get back on the shuttle."

"Lorem asked me to stay," John babbled happily. "That means I'm a permanent student at Hyperspace High."

"No way!" said Kaal, his red eyes lighting up with joy. "How on Derril did you manage that?"

"I don't know." John grinned at him. "Something about bravery. Who cares? All that matters is I don't have to go."

He felt an arm slip around his waist and looked down again into Emmie's beaming face. "That . . . is . . . *soooo* . . . cool," she said, eyes brimming with tears again. This time they were tears of happiness.

Kaal's face, meanwhile, stretched into a grin that matched John's. He threw an arm around his friend's shoulder. "Brilliant," he said. "Just brilliant. Let's go to Ska's and celebrate."

A chiming noise sounded across the deck.

John, Kaal, and Emmie looked at each other in horror. "Classes?" said Emmie. "We still have *classes?*"

"This *is* a school, Ms. Tarz," said Lorem, stepping down from the shuttle and strolling toward them. "And if my memory of the schedule is correct, you should now be on deck thirteen for an astrophysics class."

As the headmaster flashed into a ball of light, the three of them bundled into the TravelTube.

"Deck thirteen," John shouted. "*Fast!*"

"I can't wait to see Mordant's face!" Kaal shouted. "It's going to be *awesome.*"

Eyes sparkling with excitement, John grinned at his friends as Hyperspace High swept through the universe, carrying them toward distant stars and new adventures.

READ THEM ALL!

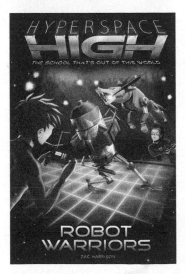
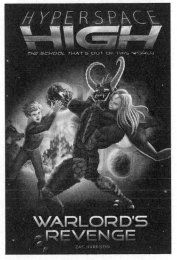